I0542557

Remka's Light

A Butler Knights Quest, Volume 1

Belenda Tonge

Published by Belenda Tonge, 2023.

This is a work of fiction. Similarities to real people, places, or events are entirely coincidental.

REMKA'S LIGHT

First edition. October 16, 2023.

ISBN: 979-8989109319

Written by Belenda Tonge.

Table of Contents

For my mother, Freida Stuber and my brother, Marshall Scott. Without their love and support, this book would not have happened.

Chapter One: Vogel's Dream

Gustav Vogel awoke with a thudding heart and labored breathing. The dream was becoming more and more real. He could see everything as if it had just happened, not 80 years ago. And yet, all it revealed was that it had been his pride that had almost killed him. But, it had also been his pride that had kept him alive. And at ninety-six years old, he knew that his time was running out. He still hadn't achieved his ultimate goal. Rich? Yes. Respected? Yes. Feared? Yes. But he did not yet possess the amulet and that he must have.

A shadow quietly entered the bedroom. Gustav knew that it was his assistant, Karl. No one else moved as he did, quiet and assured and he seemed to have a sixth sense about Gustav's health, more even than the paid nurses he had on staff.

"The dream, again, mien Herr?" Karl asked, a shaft of moonlight shining through a gap in the curtains making his silvering hair glint for an instant. He took Gustav's wrist to feel for his pulse.

"Yes," Gustav answered, shortly.

"Isn't it about time you told me what it's about?" Karl asked. "You've have me running all over the world for a decade looking for this Steadman woman, but you've never told me why. And your nightmares are becoming threats to your life. Your heart rate was much too fast this time. After all these years, don't you feel that you can trust me?"

Gustav did not reply at once, but finally nodded his head. He would need more than Karl's help. He'd need belief if Gustav were to make his journey.

"Alright, Karl. You have earned my trust many times over, so I will tell you," Gustav said. "It all began during the war."

"You were only a boy when the war started," Karl said.

"Yes, I was just eleven but I believed totally in the Reich. We'd been fed the propaganda day in and day out in school, so that's no wonder. My father was one of the holdouts and tried to discourage me from joining the Party as a youth. But, I knew that my destiny was tied into the power of the Nazis and that it was my duty to inform the authorities of my father's traitorous activities. I was fourteen when I stood next to the S.S. officer and watched as my parents were arrested. Deep inside, I felt a twinge as my mother was shoved into a canvas-covered truck, but I buried it when the S.S. officer praised me for my actions."

"What a terrible decision to have made at such a young age," Karl said, his heart aching for the boy so lost in the hysteria of the time.

"It was two years later, 1943, and I was a sixteen year old soldier in the army. I was assigned to a barracks near my father's old factory in Munich when a man dressed as a mountain peasant stepped out of a staff car and walked directly into the major's office. I was astonished that guards weren't called to drag this man out and execute him. Instead, the major called for all men with mountaineering experience and with any knowledge of Switzerland to assemble in the mess room. As I had spent summers in the Tyrolean Alps and had traveled with my parents to Lucerne many times, I followed them. The man dressed as the peasant turned out to be a colonel and he was in command of a plan to infiltrate Switzerland. I apparently answered his questions correctly as I was chosen, along with four others, to go to along with him. Two weeks later I was dressed as a herdsman walking along mountain trails, heading deep into the Swiss Alps. My mission was to find remote villages that could be infiltrated and used as staging areas for an invasion."

"There were tales of such plans to invade Switzerland. I remember my grandfather talking about it, but my mother wouldn't permit me to listen," Karl said. "She said that the war needed to be left in the past. So, what happened?"

"I discovered that the Swiss people were much more vigilant than we had thought. I spent far longer dodging their patrols than I had anticipated. A month had passed and I needed to begin the return trek or I would be left behind. That's when I found the village. It was perfect. Located in a shallow valley at the base of a granite peak with enough buildings to house a small garrison. It was isolated so that there would be few travelers passing through, especially with autumn approaching. I marked it on my map and made my way as quickly as I could back to my base.

"I didn't anticipate having a difficult time convincing the colonel that I'd found the perfect site, but he wasn't impressed. In his opinion, I was too young and inexperienced to make such a judgment. But fate intervened. Young as I was, I was the only scout to return. The other four were either captured or met with some misfortune and never returned. It was a choice of working with my intelligence, or call off the plan.

"The colonel took a middle of the road stance. He wanted to see for himself that the village was satisfactory. So, we took a small force and headed back into Switzerland. I was so proud to be leading and proud of how accurate my map was. We didn't encounter any impediments and made it to the valley in less than a week. The colonel sent men to scout the area around the village, cutting off my protest that I had already done it and there was nothing to stop us. He told me to hold my tongue and sent me to get him some food. It was a stinging insult and I'm certain he meant it to be."

"He must have been very annoyed having to take directions from a boy," Karl said.

"No doubt that was a part of it. After the scouts returned, the colonel assigned men who were to go into the village and dispose of the people. A sudden memory of my mother being arrested made me ask about the women and children.

'What about them?' the colonel responded. I knew that their fate was sealed and I felt sickened. It must have shown as the colonel sent me to watch from a ledge overlooking the village. I was to let him know when villagers were asleep. This is where my nightmare always begins.

"I was cold and shivering as I sat on the rock ledge overlooking the valley. The moon was just rising over the peaks when I saw a woman leave a cottage and run to another. She pounded on the door and when it opened, she pulled a man out and pointed to the mountain behind the village. Soon, lanterns were lit and people were gathering items into clumsy packs. Cows and goats were herded together and the entire village began to move to the base of the mountain. I was naturally curious by what they were doing, so I moved along the ledge to get a better view and be able to report to the colonel.

"What did you see?" Karl asked, intrigued with Gustav's story.

"The villagers were milling around, becoming excited. Then, from the midst of the people a woman raised her arms, commanding attention. She brought something out from under her cloak. I was too far away to see what it was, but it was small and fit into the palm of her hand. It gave off a reflected glint of moonlight as she held it up. She stooped, placed it on the ground and gave it a spin. From the center of the piece came a very small, blue glitter that began to build. It grew brighter and brighter until it was painful to look at. Then, the woman made a movement as if to gather the light and tossed it at the mountain.

"A shimmering glow began deep within the rock and it grew into the shape of an arch. Beyond the arch, seemingly within the rock, appeared a green meadow, soft and warm in sunlight. Walking toward the arch from the far end of the meadow was a dark woman. She stopped and beckoned to the people. Hesitantly, a man approached the arch, put his hand against what should have been solid rock. It went through. Startled, he pulled it back and looked at the dark woman. She beckoned again. This time, the man took one step, then another and stepped through to the other side. As one, the villagers gasped. I gasped, as well. This was unbelievable! Then the man, now on the other side of the arch beckoned. First one, then others followed him until only the woman and two small children were left, a boy of about eight years and a girl a few years younger. The girl suddenly darted back toward the village and the woman called for her to come back. I heard the boy cry that he'd get her and he ran after the child. I heard the woman scream "No!" and reach out as if to stop the children. Then, some force lifted her off from her feet and pulled her through the arch.

"The glittering light from the object suddenly flared so brightly that it dazzled my eyes, then died away completely, leaving only the light of the moon and bare rock."

"What happened to the children?" Karl asked.

"The object stopped spinning and fell over with a sharp tinkle. The little boy raced back to where the woman had been, pulling the girl by her arm. "Mama! Come back!" he shouted. The girl stooped and picked up the object the woman had set spinning. As she did so, the sound of deep, booming bells began to toll. It grew louder and louder as it echoed back and forth across the valley. I clapped my hands to my ears to try to block the sound. I saw the children huddle on the ground, their hands also clapped to their ears. I don't know how long it lasted, but it stopped as suddenly as it started. The silence stretched on and on. Then, a low rumble began and the entire valley shook. Rocks began to fall from somewhere over my head. I tried to get up and run, but a large piece of the overhang broke away and caught me, burying my legs. The pain was unbearable, but before I passed out, I saw the entire side of the mountain break off and obliterate the village. It's usually at this point that I wake up."

"It's no wonder that your heart is racing after reliving such an event," Karl said. "Perhaps your finally telling someone this story will put your dream to rest."

"Perhaps," Gustav said. "But, to continue the story, I was eventually found by some of our men and carried back to the camp. The colonel didn't want to be burdened by an injured man, so they left me by the side of a road. I was found two days later and taken to a village, then transferred to a medical facility where I was technically imprisoned. I say technically as the landslide had already imprisoned me. My lower body was paralyzed."

"Where does the Steadman woman enter into the picture?" Karl asked.

"She's the little girl who was left behind," Gustav said. "It took me years to piece the story together. The children escaped being buried by the landslide and were found wandering on a road. A family in Bern fostered them. The boy grew up, married and immigrated to the United States. His sister went with him.

"I was sent back to Munich. Years of poverty followed and I thought often that I would die. But, the memory of what I had witnessed gave me the strength to survive. Not only survive, but also to prosper. I needed to prosper because I needed to find those children. It was their mother who had roused the village. It was their mother who sent the entire village away and caused the village to be destroyed. It was she who took away my future. She owed me. Her children owed me," Gustav said, pounding his fist on the bed coverings.

"Mien Herr," Karl said, reaching to take the old man's hand. "You must calm yourself or I'll have to call for the doctor."

"No!" Gustav said. He looked into Karl's face and saw the concern reflected in his eyes. His rage dissipated and he grasped Karl's hand, seeming to gain strength through the touch. "No, Karl. I'm fine now. Let me finish."

Karl hesitated a moment feeling the tremor in Gustav's hand ease before he nodded his head, but he continued to hold the old man's hand, providing what comfort his touch could.

"I finally found where they were living in America. I traveled there, sought them out and attempted to befriend them. I told them part of my story and asked for their help. I offered them a fortune to buy the object. The brother was more than willing to sell. He'd convinced himself that their mother had died and their village wiped out in a landslide. Their mother's amulet was just an old piece of jewelry. But, the girl was different. She still had the amulet. It had been her mother's so it was beyond price. And, while she never said so, I could tell that she also knew that it was a thing of great power. Despite her brother's urging, she refused to sell it. I waited until I could speak with her alone and I begged for her help. For her to use the amulet to heal my broken body, but she refused, saying she didn't know how. Of course, I didn't believe her. I grew angry with her, frightened her. She ran away during the night."

"And this is why you've had me looking for her all these years," Karl said.

"All these years? I have spent most of my life searching for her. I am going to make her open the portal and travel through it. I know that those living there can help me. And once I am healed, I will return and get back all that should have been mine. I am going to have that amulet!"

"Mien Herr!" Karl said. "Gustav, that's," he stopped, unable to say more.

"That's what?" Gustav asked. "Insane? Of course, most people would say that. But, even though I was severely injured, I know what I saw. That woman opened a door into another place to save her people. It was a miracle and one I know I can harness."

"You had a head injury," Karl protested. "Your legs and hips were broken and your lower spine was severed. The only miracle was that you survived at all."

"Karl," Gustav said. "You are my friend, not only my friend but the son I never had. As such, you are my heir. You will inherit all my wealth when I die. I attach no caveat to this. But, I do ask you to help me. To believe that I did see something wondrous and that the means exists to create it again. Help me to find the Steadman woman and the amulet."

Karl was silent, considering his friend's request. "You are already wealthy," he said. "You have the admiration and respect of the world leaders. You are an inspiration. What more could you possibly want?"

"My destiny," Gustav said. "The destiny that was taken from me."

Karl looked at Gustav and saw the obsession in his face. He'd never seen it before. Not in all the years he'd known Gustav. It frightened Karl as nothing had before and he wondered how he could best serve the man he loved as a father. He understood that if he refused Gustav would find someone else to carry out his wishes, but they wouldn't care about the elderly man as Karl did.

"I'll continue to help," he said, at last, releasing Gustav's hand. "I have the latest report from our investigators. I gave them the information we already have, tracing the woman's movements in the United States over the course of the past sixty years. Where she moved from America to Canada to South America and back again. How she married a wealthy, American industrialist and was widowed, but had no children, and resumed her maiden name.

"Somehow, she knows she's being sought. She's successfully evaded our men and has disappeared, again. But, I have their assurance that she is somewhere on the eastern coast of the United States. Our agents will intercept her and either bring her to you or provide her location."

"Very good," Gustav said. "I am tired, Please leave me now."

"Yes, mien Herr," Karl said. He turned and left the darkened room.

Gustav waited a few moments, and then turned his head toward the door leading into his lounge. "I know you're there, Baron," he said.

The door opened immediately and a man, almost skeleton thin, with black hair and dressed in a black, silk suit entered. Gustav felt the warmth leave the room and shivered under the blankets.

"You should not have kept me waiting," the Baron said.

"I didn't send for you," Gustav said. "Why are you here?"

"To offer you my help, again," the Baron said. "Your assistant is a fool. His methods of tracing the woman will not achieve your goal. Or, should I say our goal?"

"Karl is a good man," Gustav said. "He has been with me for many years and I trust him without question as he trusts me and he is obedient to my wishes."

"He thinks that you have lost your reason," the Baron said. "He may be correct. But, there is much strength in madness as there is in fear. Strength to find and use the amulet, to use Remka's Light."

"How do you know about the amulet?" Gustav asked, becoming alarmed.

"Do you think that the enormous amount of power drawn into the amulet that was used to open the portal into Sanctuary was not felt by all who deal with the arcane?" the Baron asked. "And Remka was known from long ago. She who evaded those better suited to hold the amulet."

"Sanctuary?" Gustav pounced eagerly on that word. "Then it's truly a real place?"

"It is," the Baron answered. "And you can go there, with my help. All I ask is that I accompany you. There are many who have gone before that it would please me to gather to myself."

"It is my will that I gather the power," Gustav said.

"There is enough for both," the Baron said. "If you truly want the amulet, my Dark Hunters will find and retrieve it. You only need to say yes."

Gustav was envisioning a future where he entered Sanctuary and walked, tall and proud, again. He looked into the man's black eyes.

"Yes," he said.

"And so it will be," the Baron said. He turned and walked away from the bed and disappeared.

"And so it will be," Gustav whispered.

Chapter Two: The Ladies and the Captain

The three red haired women looked at the cargo freighter they had just purchased with satisfaction. Older and very small by comparison to the monstrous container ships that filled harbors all over the world, it was exactly what they wanted. The agent who had handled the purchase shook his head. Three women with no experience in freight, ships or international trade would be eaten alive by the competition. "Ladies, it's not too late to back out," he said. "I know of a yacht I'm sure would suit you much better."

"We appreciate your concern, but this is exactly what we want," The oldest of the three said, smiling. She was around forty with grey eyes set in a strong face. "In fact, you might say we were lead to it."

"Well, you know your own minds, I guess," he said. "I wish you the best of luck." He shook their hands then left them standing next to the gangplank. He looked back over his shoulder once. "Crazy women," he said under his breath and continued to walk away. "Wait'll they hear about this down at the union hall."

"Are you entirely certain that this is what we're supposed to do, Agnes?" the woman standing next to the eldest asked. She was thirty-five, slender with a no nonsense attitude that reflected in her granite colored eyes.

"Of course, Sofie," Agnes said. "Why do you ask?"

"Why do I ask?" Sofie repeated. "Forming a coven that travels all over the world on a tramp freighter? It's made of iron and it floats on water. Iron and water. Those are two of the big no no's to the flow of our power. And this thing looks like it'll sink any moment."

"Ask Caroline," Agnes said, nodding at her youngest sister, who at thirty still gave the impression of soft, wide-eyed innocence. "It was her vision."

"It wasn't just a vision," Caroline said. "It was a sending and a strong one. We'll need to perform a cleansing from one end to the other and seal the entire ship against both Dark forces and the draining of power. Of course we'll need to do it while the ship is in dry dock. We can't fight the influence of iron and water at the same time, even with all three of us working the spells. Then, we'll place the Rod of Compassion in the center. That's what I saw, Sofie."

"Careful about mentioning the Rod out loud," Sofie said. "You never know who might be listening."

"I'm only telling you what I saw," Caroline said.

"Alright," Agnes said. "Let's get on board and see what we have on our hands."

The three crossed from the dock onto the ship. As their feet touched the deck, they felt a decided deadening of their 'third sense,' the effect of the iron of the ship's hull blocking the earth's energy, the source of their powers.

"Ugh!" Caroline said. "Let's get this over with."

"You have the diagrams, Sofie," Agnes said. "Where should we start?"

"I'd say front to back and bottom to top," Sofie said. She dug into the large handbag she carried and pulled out three flashlights. "Here," she said handing one to each of the others. "The agent said that the generator was removed, so no lights."

Following the diagrams, they descended into the depths of the ship. Grease, grime and rust were everywhere along with the smell of fetid water and soiled living quarters. The stench emanating from the galley made them back hastily out the door with hands covering their noses.

Still, they walked the length of every deck and looked into every room and nook.

"It may be a small ship, but to me it's still massive," Sofie said several hours later, rubbing her aching feet. They were sipping tea in the living room of their hotel suite, resting after getting cleaned up.

"It'll take stacks and stacks of herb smudges and gallons of potion to make it safe for us and for the Rod, "Agnes said. "Also, we must clean and redecorate. Those staterooms are an absolute disgrace and I don't even want to think about the kitchen and dining room. I felt like I needed to burn my clothes what with the smell clinging to them, not to mention the smears of grease and rust. I can't believe that all that deterioration only happened after the ship was taken out of service. It's a wonder that the crew didn't come down with typhoid or something. We'll never get customers if word gets out about what a shamble things are."

"It's called a galley, not a kitchen and I don't think anyone we rescue will care, as long as they're safe," Sofie said. "But you're right. If we're to live on board we'll have to have things clean and there must be some comforts. And not just for us. We'll need to think about our coven members, too. They won't be able to do their jobs if they're stressed. I wonder how one goes about finding an interior decorator for a ship?"

Agnes and Sofie laughed, but Caroline remained silent, eyes unfocused.

"Caroline?" Sofie asked softly. "What do you see?"

"There's a man coming," Caroline said. She was a petite woman with long, ruddy red hair and very pale skin due to the fact that she rarely stayed long outside. Her cloud grey eyes often appeared glazed, but in reality, she was immersed in the unseen, seeking those in need of their specialized form of help. "He's lost, depressed and at the end of his strength. He's the one we need. He has gifts but he is not a practicing Wielder of the Power. We must tread carefully until he gains understanding, but betrayal is not within him." She shook her head and refocused on her sisters, then looked at the telephone sitting on the end table. It rang and Agnes reached over to answer it.

"Miss Butler," a man's voice said. "This is Robert at the front desk. There's a man here requesting to see you. Are you expecting anyone?"

"We are indeed," Agnes said. "Please send him right up, Robert."

"Yes, Miss Butler," Robert said. "It's just that he's somewhat-"

"Send him up," Agnes interrupted. "We don't judge books by their covers. Also, please have room service send up four complete dinner specials with lots of coffee."

"Yes, Miss Butler," he said.

A knock announced the arrival of their guest and Sofie opened the door. Standing on the threshold was a man around thirty-five years old. He was a bit shorter than average with blond hair in need of a clip. He appeared somewhat gaunt, as if he hadn't been eating well or often and while clean, his clothes were a bit threadbare. But his blue eyes were clear and bright with no trace of either alcohol or drugs. It was a good sign.

"Excuse me, ma'm," he said. "Are you Ms. Butler? The new owner of the Happenstance?"

"I am, one of them. And you are?"

"Name's Nolan," he said. "Kyle Nolan."

"Please come in, Mr. Nolan," Sofie said, stepping aside for him to enter the room. "These are my sisters," she said. "Agnes, Caroline, and I'm Sofie. We did indeed purchase the Happenstance. What may we do for you?

"Word's out that you're planning to put the old girl back in commission," he said. "Is that true?"

"Yes, it is," Sofie said. "We were going over the ship's layout just this afternoon to determine what we'll need. What is your interest?"

"Word's also out that you don't know the bridge from a barnacle about ships," he said.

"I take it that you do?" Agnes said, trying not to smile.

"Yes, I do," he said. "You're going to need a good crew if you're going to go blindly into the shipping business. There're many who'll take you for everything you've got, including the ship. You'll need help."

"Are you offering to help?" Sofie asked.

"I'm looking for work," he said. "I can do anything required from deckhand to machinist and I won't cheat you."

"You're an officer," Caroline said.

The man didn't say anything for a moment then he straightened his shoulders and looked directly at her. "I was," he said. "You may as well know. I was the first officer on the Happenstance before the owners took her out of service. The captain, well he wasn't the most trustworthy of officers."

"He was drunk on duty and passed out," Caroline interrupted. "He never heard the lookout's call about the sailboat in the path of the ship. Two people were killed when the ship struck their boat. He put the blame on you."

"He said that I was late for duty as I was the one who was drunk," Nolan said, a bitter set to his face. "It was a flat out lie, but the owners believed him, not me. As a result, no one would hire me. And, as the family of the two who'd died was suing, the owners decided to get rid of the ship." He looked at the faces studying him. His lips thinned as he realized that the women had obviously heard the gossip. He'd been a fool to come.

"I'm sorry to have bothered you," he said, standing up, preparing to leave.

"Where are you going?" Sofie asked. "You said you were looking for work and we're in need of a captain."

He starred at her in disbelief. "Are you saying you'll hire me? Even knowing about me?"

"You're innocent of any wrongdoing, aren't you?" Agnes asked. "You must know the ship inside and out and you know about how the shipping business works. What else do we need to know?"

A knock on the door interrupted further conversation. "Room service," a voice announced.

"Good," Agnes said. "I'm hungry. You'll join us, Captain Nolan?" She indicated a seat at the table. Dumbfounded, he followed her and found a plate with a steak, baked potato and green beans placed in front of him. He looked around the table at the three women and wondered what possessed them to buy a ship they were ill equipped to handle. He sensed that there was something more about the situation than just three 'crazy women' throwing their money away. And, he also wondered what possessed him to seek them out. He'd heard the laughter of the able bodied seamen when they'd learned about the purchase of the ship. He hadn't joined in. The Happenstance had been home but there was something more, something that pulled at him. He just didn't know exactly what it was.

The dinner conversation centered on the ship. They discussed her present condition and what it would take to get her ready to sail. He was able to answer every question the women posed and as he showed his knowledge they appeared more and more pleased. In turn, he began to feel that these women weren't as innocent or incompetent as they appeared. Their questions showed a subtle understanding of the ship and maritime laws.

"Well, I'm satisfied," Agnes said after draining her coffee cup and pushing her chair back from the table. "Sofie? Caroline?" Both of the sisters nodded in agreement. "So, do we say welcome aboard, Captain Nolan?"

"I don't know how to thank you," he said. He felt good. Better than he had in months. The prospect of commanding the Happenstance was like slipping into a place waiting for him.

"Don't thank us, yet," Sofie said. "You may not want the job after you see who we are and what we intend to do."

"Sofie," Agnes said with a warning glance.

"Not smugglers," he said, suddenly uneasy. "I won't work with smugglers."

"No, we're not smugglers," Sofie said, smiling. "Believe it or not, we're witches."

Nolan didn't say anything but he felt like he'd been punched in the gut. He stood and calmly walked to the door.

"Oh, dear," Agnes said. "Caroline said we'd have to go easy. We shouldn't have just sprung it on him. Looks like we'll need to prove it. Sofie?"

Sofie waved her hand and the lock on the door turned. Nolan tried to unlock it but it wouldn't budge. "Alright," he snarled. "What's the deal?"

"Watch," Sofie said. She waved her hand again. The dishes they'd just eaten from levitated off the table and floated over to the serving cart the steward had left in the corner. A glow developed around of the flower vase in the center of the table. Caroline, who had remained seated stared into it.

"Captain Nolan," she said. "You left home at the age of fourteen after the death of your parents. You'd been placed with your uncle who was violently abusive toward you. You made your way to the coast where you had always been most at ease. There, you were taken in by an old seaman whom you called Pops. He made a home for you, sent you to school and taught you a trade. You rapidly rose in rank from apprentice seaman to first officer. Pops gave you the medals he'd won while in the Navy to show you how proud he was of you. He passed on before the incident aboard the Happenstance. You were glad he hadn't lived to see your fall from grace."

"Captain," Agnes said. "No doubt you think that we're insane. That we rigged the room with parlor tricks and had you investigated so that we could impress you with knowledge of your past. Certainly, we could have done that. But, ask yourself why. Why would we? How could we even know that you'd come to see us? We didn't need to tell you anything about us. We could have discussed your salary and duties and how best to get the Happenstance ready to sail and not make you think you'd run into three deranged females."

"So, why did you?" Nolan asked his eyes narrowed with suspicion. He moved to keep as much distance between himself and the women as the room permitted. He wasn't a fan of crazy, especially when he seemed to have stepped right into the middle of it.

"We've been given a mission," Caroline said. "There are those of the Power who are in danger. Evil forces are ever greedy for new energy. They seek out those who either Wield or Guard focuses of the Power of Light so that they can absorb their power. We've been charged with finding those who need help and to bring them to safety, to a new life, protected by those gifts that we hold. There was a Sending from the Power telling us that we're to create a coven, a circle of those who will rescue these Children of the Light as knights of old were believed to save the innocent."

"Caroline had a vision," Agnes said. "It foretold that you would come to us. We need you to become a central figure within our circle. To head the non-occult activities, keeping the ship running, overseeing cargos and passengers like a normal tramp freighter and to maintain our cover. Meanwhile, we handle the sorcery side of things. What do you say?"

Nolan didn't trust himself to speak. He felt dizzy. He needed to get out of the room and clear his head. The food. He'd obviously been drugged. That was the only explanation for these demented ramblings. Fresh air. He needed fresh air.

Sofie had been watching him closely and waved her hand again. The door unlocked and swung open. Nolan almost stumbled in his haste to leave. He all but ran down the hotel hallway to reach the stairs, not daring to wait for the elevator.

"Well, that's that," Sofie said. "We'll just have to look for someone else. Pity, he'd have been an excellent choice."

"No," Caroline said. "The vision didn't lie. He'll return."

The next morning, there was a knock at the door. This time, Agnes answered it. Nolan stood there. "I think you three ladies are crazy. But if you are I must be, too," he said. "I had a dream last night where I was the captain of the Happenstance. A great voice spoke to me and said that I must help you. That danger would challenge us, but that if we remained true to our cause, we'd lead a good life and help many people. I woke up with such an urge to get started, I almost ran out without getting dressed. I don't understand it but if you still want me, here I am."

"Excellent, Captain," Agnes said, smiling. "Caroline said that you had some gifts. Your receiving a sending proves that. Give us a few minutes and we'll be ready to leave. You can go over the ship and tell us what's needed to get it ready to sail. We'll take care of the protections and of course, refurbishing the cabins and crew quarters."

"Protections?" Nolan asked.

"Protections from the Dark Ones," she said. "It's best if we do that when the ship's in dry dock."

Nolan shook his head. The more he thought about what he was getting into, the more insane it seemed.

"Perhaps we should create a To Do list," Sofie said. She was a firm believer in making lists.

"It'll take more than a list," Nolan said. "We don't even know if the previous owners left her sea worthy. They were going to sell her for scrap, so most of the usable equipment has likely been stripped and while those can be replaced, the first concern must be the hull. X-rays to find any cracks or weak places and an overall inspection. Cleaning and redecorating and protections, or whatever, are last."

"Excellent," Sofie said. "Who should we call for this service?"

"Um, Ladies," Nolan said, a slight frown forming between his eyes. "You understand that this is going to be extremely expensive. Not just the hull, but there's the engines, the props, the pumps and that's just the beginning. The integrity of the bulkheads, the decks and the cargo holds. Anything that isn't sea worthy must be replaced for everyone's safety. There's also the dry dock rental. The costs will be enormous. It's why almost all shipping companies are corporations with stockholders and not individuals. The purchase of the ship alone would bankrupt most people. Forgive me for prying into your finances, but you'll need to be certain of your access to adequate funds before you even begin."

"You don't need to worry about funds," Agnes said. "Let's just say that we inherited family wealth and have amazing advice for investments. We're financially secure enough to handle the costs."

Nolan studied the women for several moments. Agnes and Sofie both had small, serene smiles while Caroline glanced down, moving her hands restlessly across the top of the table.

"If you can afford to rehab an old tub like the Happenstance, why not buy a new vessel?" he asked.

"Because we were sent to rescue the ship," Caroline said. "The Happenstance is, or will be, a container of the Power. It will be our home and our fortress."

"Caroline has foreseen this and we never doubt the dictates of the Powers of Light," Agnes said.

"Okay then. Let's get this show on the road," Sofie said, picking up a notepad and pen. "You were going to tell us whom to contact about inspecting the hull."

Nolan again shook his head in wonder. It was something he would do many times in the months to come. He sighed and began to provide a list of the names of the companies they'd need to contact.

Chapter Three: The Happenstance Awakens

It took the better part of the year to refurbish the Happenstance. Nolan and the Ladies stood on the bridge that was sparkling clean, freshly painted and polished to within an inch.

"It hardly seems real," Nolan said. "When I think about how she was when we began, I doubted she'd ever be ready to put to sea again."

"Yes," Agnes said. "It's been quite a journey. I have to admit that I had no idea of how much effort it would take to transform the pile of junk we bought into a sea worthy vessel."

Nolan nodded his head. He remembered how his stomach had knotted up when he saw the Happenstance for the first time since his dismissal. Peeling paint and rust everywhere. This wasn't the ship he remembered. He'd stroked the railing when he stepped aboard as if to reassure the ship of the group's intentions.

They'd gone through the ship much more thoroughly than the Ladies had before. Nolan knew where every piece of equipment went and what was missing or appeared damaged. It made an extensive list. His experienced eye also noted dents in the bulkheads and places that would need major repairs.

"Well, what is our first task?" Sofie asked.

"The hull," Nolan said. "X-rays and replacement of any sections that show cracks or are damaged. The hull is our first and only protection from the sea. Nothing else matters if the hull isn't intact."

And so it began. Every section of the hull was examined and almost all were replaced. The bulkheads were subjected to the same rigorous inspection and replacement. It seemed as if the lightening bright flares of the welding torches and the smell of molten metal would never end.

Next came the engines and propulsion system and more welding along with replacing pumps and electric cables throughout the entire ship. Watertight doors, deck plating and equipment to handle cargo were installed. It was a massive effort and as the seasons changed from summer to autumn then to winter, storms often caused delays. The Ladies discussed the frequency and severity of the storms and questioned if they were natural. There was nothing to do but keep working.

Each of the four found a way for their talents to contribute. Nolan had the technical knowledge and as the captain he would not sign off on any work unless it was the best possible. Agnes and Sofie made certain that the work remained organized and Caroline provided emotional support that kept everyone calm. But, all of them were directly involved with rolled up sleeves and coated with grime at the end of each day.

Finally, the last weld was made, the final coat of paint was applied and the last circuit was installed. Now came the cleansing and sealing the ship against both evil forces and the draining of Power. Each compartment was scrubbed to remove any physical dirt then cleansed with potion, herb smudges and spell castings. This only the Ladies could do and they had to perform their castings during the last hours before dawn.

"I thought that evil spells were made at night," Nolan said. "Why aren't you doing your spells during the day?"

"Night isn't necessarily evil," Caroline said. "And day isn't necessarily good. They just are. The time between moon set and sunrise is a time of balance. We use this balance to release any negative forces existing within the ship and to invite positive forces to fill the voids."

"We also don't want any of the workmen to see what we are doing," Agnes said. "We've had more than enough gossip and we don't want to draw the attention of any Dark Ones who might sabotage our efforts."

"Should we post a guard?" Nolan asked.

"No, that would only confirm that we're up to something," Sofie said.

It took another month to get the cleansing and sealing completed but when it was finished, even Nolan could feel the difference.

Nolan took one last look around the bridge before he issued his first order. He picked up a telephone and pushed a button to call the engine room. "Start the engines," he said to the temporary engineer who had answered. He and the Ladies all cheered as the engines roared to life. "She's back," Nolan said. "She's alive, again."

"Not entirely," Agnes said. "But, it's a beginning. Now for the coven members."

Chapter Four: The Knights Assemble

"We need to discuss hiring a crew," Agnes said over their breakfast table. It had been two days since they had started the Happenstance's engines and it was time to get her out of dry dock.

"There'll be a lot of initial interest down at the union hall," Nolan said. "The sales agent made sure of that. But, once they find out about you and your plans, you won't find a single man willing to ship out with you. Seamen tend to be superstitious."

"Huh! I never thought of that," Agnes said. "There could be friction between the crew and the coven. That'll never do."

"Do we need to have both crew and coven members? Couldn't they be one and the same?" Caroline asked.

"Coven members performing crew tasks? They'd never go along with that," Agnes said.

"Why not?" Nolan asked. "None of you were too good to get your hands dirty. Why should you bring aboard anyone who wouldn't do likewise?"

"I've been giving it some thought," Sofie said. "It should be simple enough. We'll advertise for those we'll need."

"Advertise?" Nolan asked. "You mean like 'wanted, crew to man witches' ship'?"

Sofie and Agnes laughed. "Something like that," Sofie said. "We can place a spell on the advertisements so that only those with the correct gifts of power and would be willing to take on ship's duties will even see them. Of course, we'll post hiring notices and interview regular crews so no one will notice that we all of a sudden have a full complement. We can take care of the interviewing so you won't need to be involved and feel awkward about discussing gifts."

"Ladies, you need to understand that as captain, I hold the responsibility for the ship's safety," Nolan said. "That said I must approve all decisions about the ship, the crew, cargos and destinations."

"Indeed?" Agnes asked, eyes snapping in anger.

"There can only be one captain, ladies," he said. "We need to establish this right off or call it quits, at least as far as my being captain is concerned. You're the owners but it must be me who makes the final decisions about the crew."

"He's right, Agnes," Caroline said. "We need to focus on finding and helping those at risk, not running a ship. We can't proceed with our mission if our attention is split."

Agnes took a deep breath and nodded her head. "Alright, you're the captain."

"In case you didn't notice it, Agnes has a bit of a temper," Sofie said, turning her attention to Nolan. "Try not to get her riled up unless you're interested in life as a rabbit or a frog."

"She can really do that?" Nolan asked.

None of the women replied, but Agnes just smiled and tilted her head to one side. "Let's get busy," she said.

The hiring notices did garner quite a bit of interest from the locals and each was duly interviewed and advised that they would be notified when a decision was made. But, it was the advertisements that appeared in every newspaper and on every applicable website that brought those with the gifts the sisters were looking for.

In spite of what he'd been told, Nolan was surprised that each applicant also brought a needed skill to the ship's crew compliment. He personally selected a man from Galveston, Texas named Gordon Pierce as first officer, in spite of some reservations about his other skills dealing with animals, especially snakes and reptiles and his insistence on keeping a boa constrictor he called Myra in his stateroom.

A man named Umar Kambuto was selected as boatswain. Tall, dark and unsmiling, he projected an ominous air that no deckhand could ignore, even if they wanted to. He was the equivalent to any of the Ladies in Power and with the gift of clairvoyance. He confronted Dark forces without fear. None of the deckhands went out of their way to try and be friendly with him until a man from Veracruz, Mexico named Miguel Vargas arrived. Short, thin, with black hair and dark eyes that sparkled with merriment, he was the polar opposite of the African. Yet, they took a great liking to each other, which was a good thing as their mystical gifts complimented each other well. Miguel was descended from a Mayan priest and was a fierce fighter when confronted by evil. They would often find themselves teamed up for rescue missions.

Captain Nolan was still uncertain about the dual purpose of the ship, but three months later, the Happenstance was ready to sail. Only one thing remained, setting the Rod of Compassion. The three Butler sisters invited the Captain and the crewmembers, those they now called their Knights, to attend the ceremony. This would formalize the creation of the coven. Each of the Knights wore a ring with a glowing green stone in the center that Sofie had created and enchanted. Deep within the ship at the exact center, the three women walked in a circle around a golden rod set upright in a base of alabaster and inscribed with many symbols. Each woman carried an artifact. Agnes held a rounded piece of amber with leaves encased in the middle. Sofie held a slender piece of oak with a gold tip affixed to one end. Finally, Caroline carried a fist-sized globe of crystal that pulsed with a pure, white light.

"By the Fire, by the Water, by the Earth and Air," they intoned. "With the setting of this Rod, we offer compassion to all we encounter. Let none be left in danger, bereft or in want. With harm to none, so do we dedicate our lives and our powers."

Without understanding why, Nolan, along with the others, held their ringed hands toward the rod and repeated the last line of the incantation, sealing them to the Happenstance, to its mission and to the Butler Knights.

Chapter Five: The Cairo Capper

First officer Pierce, Umar and Miguel crouched behind a boulder on a hill overlooking the compound of Giles Tolliver, a smuggler and gunrunner. The waning moon wouldn't give enough light for them to see their way down the slope, but that didn't matter. Torches blazed inside and all around the walls. Armed guards were stationed at various points and were clearly visible. Barely fifty miles from the very modern metropolis of Cairo, Egypt, Tolliver had built himself a veritable fortress.

"He's set himself up like a feudal lord," Miguel said. "Look at all that firepower the guards are carrying." He suddenly stiffened. Something was crawling across the back of his leg. "Ah, Mr. Pierce," he said.

"Hold very still," Umar said. "It's an Egyptian cobra."

Pierce turned to gaze at the snake that was starting to coil next to Miguel's leg. He took a breath and his Knight ring began to softly glow green. "Go hunt elsewhere," he said, his voice barely above a whisper. "Nothing for you here little one." He flicked a finger at the snake and watched as it slithered away into the dark.

Miguel let out the breath he had been holding and he shuddered. "No offense, Mr. Pierce," he said. "But I really, really hate snakes."

"I thought you were descended from a Mayan priest," Pierce said. "Didn't they believe that snakes were sacred?"

"They did, but not me," Miguel said.

"Shoot, son" Pierce said in an exaggerated Texas drawl. "Back home, we got rattlers so big they'd make that cobra look like a night crawler."

"Listen!" Umar said.

The sound of a truck engine could be heard approaching, the grinding of its gears discernible in the clear dessert air.

"That must be our thief coming to present the orb to Tolliver," Pierce said. He raised the binoculars he'd worn around his neck and watched the truck bounce over the rutted, dirt road that served the compound. As it came close to the iron gate, a guard halted it and spoke with the driver. Other guards opened the back of the truck and hauled a small, thin man out, shoving him to the front of the truck where the head guard could look at him.

"Yes," Pierce said. "There's Philippe. He doesn't have the cane, so he must have removed the orb."

"I hope that those guards don't search him and keep it for themselves," Miguel said.

"Unless they have a death wish, they won't," Umar said. "Tolliver isn't a forgiving man and would make quite an example of any of his men who might steal it from him."

"Let's hope that none of them find out the true nature of the orb," Pierce said. "Tolliver thinks that he's going to acquire a pretty, new toy. A gem he can gloat over. But if he ever discovers what the orb really is and what it can do, he'd go mad with greed."

"How could Jean Duval have put the orb into such a vulnerable situation where it could be stolen by a second rate thief?" Miguel asked. "Why couldn't he just stay safely in his Parisian bistro and tell fortunes instead of going to a back alley casino? He was making a bundle from his clients."

"Those are excellent questions," Umar said. "And ones I'm certain our Ladies have asked. In fact, I know that Miss Sofie was ready to scorch Duval's goatee off for his unheard of lack of judgment. After all, the Ladies depend on his visions for their financial investments."

"Look," Pierce said. "The guards are letting Philippe in. Time for our delivery."

Umar nodded and disappeared into the night leaving Pierce and Miguel to make their way down the slope and hide behind a boulder next to the road.

Shortly, the sound of another engine growled toward the fortress gates. The small, old van they had borrowed from a food provisioner based in Cairo came into view and Umar was driving. He stopped at the gate and got out when the guard pointed an automatic rifle at him.

"Who are you and where is Asim?" the guard asked.

"My much revered master is ill," Umar replied. "He had the order for the lord Tolliver ready and knew that much displeasure would befall if the delivery was late. So, I am sent. There is much food and drink. Look! Look! There is enough for all."

The other guards had opened the doors of the van and were handing out bottles of wine, laughing at the dismay Umar was feigning. "That is the lord Tolliver's wine," Umar said. "He will be very angry and so will my master."

"Go on," the head guard said. "Make your delivery. The lord Tolliver will never miss these few bottles."

Umar jumped back into the van and drove through the gates. He stopped the van near a door where another guard was waving. Again, he had to explain about his poor ill master and the urgency of the completed delivery.

"Yes, yes," the guard said. "Now unload that van and stack everything inside the storeroom. And, I'll want to count every box and crate. I know how you cheat."

"Yes, effendi," Umar said, bowing as he opened the van's door. "There is no cheat. See? I stack the boxes."

"What's this?" the guard asked pointing at the wine crate the gate guards had opened. "You stole some of Tolliver's wine!"

"No! No, effendi," Umar protested. "I do not steal. The other guards, they take the wine and drink it. Go! Look and see." Umar pretended fear of the guard's reaction but was ready to throw a protection spell if the guard made a move to strike out with the butt of his rifle.

"Oh, they did, did they?" the guard said, a slow smile forming on his lips. "Smart men. I think the rest of us deserve our share of these of these bottles. You finish unloading the rest of this stuff and get going. And, you better keep your mouth shut."

"Yes, effendi," Umar said. "For certain. I hear and see nothing."

"Good man," the guard said, and laughed.

Umar took his time unloading the van, waiting for the sleeping potion they'd injected into the wine bottles to take effect. He hoped that it would be soon so that Pierce and Miguel could enter the compound. Outside the walls, Pierce and Miguel watched from cover as the guards began to stagger and one by one, fell over. They waited until they saw Umar open the gate and wave at them to enter.

"Tolliver's living quarters are over in the main building. Philippe must also be there," Umar said, pointing at a square, two-story building that looked like it had been constructed for a movie set. The three men ran swiftly across the open compound and up a set of steps to a verandah. They inched over to a lit window and looked inside. There they saw a bald, middle-aged man sitting on what was almost a throne. Without a doubt, this must be Tolliver. At his feet knelt their thief holding a black, velvet bag. Pierce held up his hand to his ear, the green stone in his Knight ring glowing. He tilted his head to listen.

"Here is the item we discussed, Monsieur," Philippe said. "A beautiful gem, the size of a hen's egg." He opened the bag and spilled the contents into his hand. He held the orb up so that the light made the facets sparkle. "As you can see, it is without flaw, magnificent, beyond price. But, of course, there is the price we discussed." He closed his hand over the orb and waited for Tolliver's reaction.

"You will be paid," Tolliver said. "After the gem has been authenticated. Tell me how you acquired this bauble"

"Bauble Monsieur?" Philippe asked. Acting offended, he stood up and made to put the orb back into the bag. "I tell you that this diamond is reputed to have belonged to Tsar Nicholas of Russia and was smuggled out during the revolution."

"I'm sure," Tolliver said. "Just as sure that you actually brought me a real diamond. In other words, mon ami, not at all."

"Monsieur!" Philippe said but stopped as he realized that Tolliver held a small pistol and that it was pointed directly at him.

"Hand me the gem," Tolliver said. "I don't want to damage it when I shoot you."

"But, it is real, I tell you," Philippe said. "Just maybe not from Russia. I took it from the old fortuneteller in Paris I told you about. He was using it as the head of his walking stick, but everyone knew it was a real diamond."

The three men had heard enough and knew that Tolliver would kill Philippe. They ran to the door and threw their combined weight against it. The door burst open. As a practiced team, Umar and Miguel both waved their hands feeling the power build, Umar's like ice and Miguel's like fire, each feeding it into their Knight rings. They aimed the rings and sent blasts of power at Tolliver and Philippe, knocking them to the floor. Pierce ran across the room and grabbed the velvet bag from Philippe's hand then ran back to the door. Umar and Miguel followed before Tolliver could find his gun and fire at them.

"Guards!" Tolliver yelled. "Guards, intruders in the compound! Guards!"

Pierce and Miguel hopped into the back of the van while Umar got behind the wheel and started the engine. "Hold on," he yelled. Kicking up a spray of gravel, the van roared toward the gates and hit them, knocking them wide open. Pierce and Miguel were tossed around as the van swayed over the rutted road heading back to Cairo.

Umar drove with the intensity of someone being chased. Once they'd made it to the paved highway, they made good time but when Pierce looked out through the back window, he saw that they actually were being chased. It was close to midnight and there wasn't much traffic this far away from the city center. The headlights of the vehicle behind them kept getting closer.

Umar drove as fast as the old van could go, but it was no match for the Hummer that was about to overtake it. They'd made it to the outskirts of Cairo and began to look for streets narrow enough that the van could pass through but which might not accommodate the larger vehicle following them.

"Ahead, on the left," Pierce said.

Umar nodded and waited until the last moment before making the sharp turn. He drove partway down the street then stopped. The three men jumped out and began running, leaving the van to block the road. They heard the crash when their pursuers' Hummer smashed into the van and pushed it into a building. Loud cries from people who began streaming out of their homes followed as the Knights ran down the street. They made a turn that would take them west toward the Giza plateau and where they hoped they could find a main street and a taxi. But, before they made it too far, the sounds of gunfire made them stop. Turning back, they found Tolliver, one of his guards and Philippe all pointing guns at them.

"You lead us a merry chase, gentlemen," Tolliver said. "But, it was a lost cause from the start. No one steals from me and gets away with it. I do congratulate you on your cleverness in drugging most of my guards. As you can see, it was necessary for me to draft this nasty, little ferret to assist me with reclaiming my property which he will now do." He motioned for Philippe to search the men.

Before Philippe could get close enough to touch him, Umar raised his hands higher and taking a deep breath he uttered a word of command. "Kizuizi!" Philippe hit the barrier Umar had just place in front of them. Miguel's hands made a rolling motion forming a ball of power ready to toss, his eyes on the guns aimed at the Knight team. Meanwhile, Pierce reached out, curling his fingers as if to gather something. Out of the yards, streets and gutters slithered a mass of snakes collecting between the barrier and Tolliver and his men. Philippe screamed, turned and ran past Tolliver, bowling over the guard in his haste to get away. The guard regained his feet and threw his gun at the snakes before following Philippe. Tolliver showed his courage and stood his ground.

"I don't know how you did this, but I'll tell you that this is not over," Tolliver said. "I will have my men covering every way out of the city. They'll find you before the sun rises. I will have that gem and there is nothing you can do to prevent it. If nothing else, I'll take it from the old fortune teller's dead hand, should you manage to return it to him."

None of the men responded to Tolliver and after another moment, he turned and walked away. Pierce's arms were shaking with the effort it took to hold the snakes. He slowly opened his hands releasing and dispersing the snakes. Umar waited until the road was clear before letting the barrier drop. His face was streaked with sweat, but otherwise showed no sign of strain.

Miguel released the power he'd been holding in a shower of sparkles. "That was a close call," he said.

"Too close," Pierce said. He held up his left arm showing the others a hole in his shirtsleeve that had been torn by one of the bullets. "Let's get out of here." They started walking again, hoping to find a taxi and get to the rail station.

Thanks to the potion in the wine, Tolliver was unable to send any of his men to stop them from leaving Cairo and getting to the port in Alexandria. An official with the port authority made a half-hearted attempt to keep the Happenstance from leaving, but some pound notes passed between him and Captain Nolan took care of that inconvenience.

A short stop at the port of Marseilles, with a quick side trip to Paris completed the Knights' mission but not for the Ladies. They called a meeting with Nolan, Pierce, Umar and Miguel.

"We need to discuss how we can do better," Agnes said. "Retrievals like this one where you were forced to physically assault non-magical people and literally snatch the orb from their hands put you in too much risk of exposure. People like Philippe will talk and Tolliver will be giving thought as to how you used your gifts and how he could get his hands on them. Also, such a story will eventually reach the ears of a practitioner of the Dark."

"There was no other way, Miss Agnes," Pierce said. "Tolliver had a gun on Philippe and he was going to shoot. It would have been better if we could've talked Philippe into giving us the orb before he arrived in Cairo, but only fear of us might have been able to get through to him. We just didn't have time."

"What we need is someone with the ability of persuasion," Caroline said.

"Yes," Umar said. "Someone who could specialize in gaining the trust of others. Both those who are magical and those who are not."

"Well, it looks as if we need a new crew member," Nolan said. "I really don't want to have anyone facing both a practitioner of the Dark and a bullet."

"Agreed," Sofie said. "So, what type of crew member do we need to advertise for, Captain?"

Nolan smiled and looked at the coffee cup he'd been holding. "Cook has asked me about getting him some help in the kitchen. What about a ship's steward?"

"Good idea," Agnes said. "Sofie can draft up one of our special advertisements and get it sent out before we leave port. Our new member should be waiting for us when we reach the States."

Chapter Six: A Distressed Damsel

"Caroline's had a foretelling," Sofie said, stepping into the ship's galley. "We have a new rescue."

"Oh?" Agnes asked, stirring a large cast iron pot sitting on the stove. "Who and where?"

"She says it's a Guardian," Sofie said. That was important. Guardians were more at risk than Wielders. They didn't have the option of using the power of the objects they held in trust to protect themselves from evil. Wielders could, so weren't usually targeted that much. At least, they hadn't been until recently. There seemed to have been a shift in the forces that was troubling. Knight teams had been sent to rescue three Wielders during the past year. Word had spread in the magical community that it would be prudent to stay out of sight.

"It's a woman and she's currently at the Boston safe house," Sofie said.

As Boston had a long history of arcane events, it was decided that it would be the homeport for the Happenstance. It had also been decided that it would be prudent to establish a land-based refuge for their rescued parties and artifacts. They even had a web site under the name of 'The Butler Knights Magical Rescue and Retrieval Foundation.' Agnes felt that a foundation gave a sense of credibility. Sofie crafted a spell that only permitted those who needed the Knights' help access to the computer link.

"We need to get a team out right away," Sofie said. She reached out to push a lose hairpin back into the fiery red bun atop Agnes's head. She preferred to keep her darker red curls short. It was much more efficient.

"Alright," Agnes said, wiping perspiration from her brow with her sleeve. "Let me finish my potion while you call Caroline, the Captain, Mr. Kambuto and Mr. Jones to the situation room."

"Are you sure you want Rolland Jones?" Sofie asked. "We've only had him for six months. He can barely cast a simple protection spell and Caroline said the situation is urgent. Maybe we should send Mr. Vargas instead, or at least have him go along."

"No," Agnes said. "Rollie needs to take this one. I know it'll be dangerous, but aren't they all? He needs to know that he can handle things. Otherwise, he'll never become the extraction specialist we needed. After all, he did answer our ad."

Sofie nodded, not entirely convinced, but she didn't argue. Their recovery job in Cairo had convinced them that they needed someone with Mr. Jones' abilities. She just hoped he was the right person for this rescue. She left to gather the individuals Agnes named while Agnes began to ladle hot, greenish liquid into brown bottles.

"I'll be back to finish up after we get the team going," Agnes said to the white-coated cook who'd been standing behind her.

"Got a new case, eh?" he asked. "Will the team need any food supplies to go?"

I'm not certain," she said. "Maybe something they can slip into a pocket and eat on the run. High-energy, protein bars."

"Right," he said. "I'll see to it."

"Thank you," Agnes said as she hurried out the door.

The situation room was actually one of the smaller crew cabins. It was located across from the captain's cabin near the bridge of the freighter. It contained a table and half a dozen chairs. There was a window covered with light blue curtains and beige carpeting on the floor. There was nothing to indicate that there was anything special about the room. Nothing that is, until one stepped across the threshold and felt the sharp tingle of the multiple spells placed around the room. One invoked privacy. No one outside could see into the room or hear what those inside said. Another blocked anyone not specifically invited from entering and for added measure, a third acted as a curtain so that the room became unnoticeable after the last invitee entered. Sofie specialized in spell casting and invoked these after Agnes called for the meeting. Agnes usually brewed up the potions they used while Caroline was the seer of the group.

"So, Caroline," Agnes said. "Please bring everyone up to speed on our newest rescue."

"A Guardian has been Sent to our safe house in Boston," Caroline said. The others in the room shifted uncomfortably. A Sending usually meant big trouble with a Dark force. "Jay Danvers was working late in the focus repository, so had to handle things. But there were too many Dark Hunters for him to handle by himself and her location won't remain secret for long. We need to get her out and under the protection of a Knight team P.D.Q."

"Yes," Sofie said. "There's no better object curator than Jay. His skill at verification, cataloging and sealing away the orphaned objects of Power we've retrieved from the Dark is second to none, but direct confrontation? Definitely, not his forte."

"Do you want to move the ship to the Boston port?" Captain Nolan asked the women. The ship had a paying cargo consigned to go to London. A part of his responsibility was to oversee the money making end of things and keep up the appearance that the Happenstance was just another tramp freighter while the 'Ladies Butler' were doing their magical rescues. He sometimes felt as if he were living in two very different worlds at the same time. One was the real, hard working world of a seafarer and the other, a fantasy world full of sorcery. He was never sure which one he was in at any given time.

"I don't think we should," Caroline said. "It would take too long. We can fly a team in and bring her back before we could get the ship out of New York and we can't use the Power travel spell this close to a port."

"Alright then," Agnes said. "Mr. Jones will go in for the extraction and Mr. Kambuto will provide security. Let's get you going."

Rollie looked at Umar Kambuto and found him looking back. Rollie was short, on the scrawny side, with light brown hair, brown eyes and had a slight gap in his upper front teeth that showed often as he smiled often. The son of a psychiatrist mother and a police detective father, he'd grown up wanting to be a private investigator. He hadn't known he was gifted until the Ladies advertisement for a ship's steward brought him from Indiana. Six months of tutelage with the Ladies had given him an idea of what he was supposed to be capable of, but he hadn't been tested. Umar was tall and lanky with very dark skin and eyes that observed everything. An African mystic had trained him from childhood. From the stories told about him, he was as formidable as the Ladies. Several hours later, they arrived at the Knight's Boston safe house.

"I'll keep watch and you go in and try to convince her to come with us," Umar said. "And hurry. I have a feeling that we don't have much time for discussion."

"Right," Rollie said. He lightly ran up the front steps and rang the doorbell. A stout man dressed in a grey sweat suit answered. Rollie held up his right hand and his ring flashed green. This was both a symbol of a Knight member and a protection for the wearer. The man responded in kind and held open the door.

"I'm Rollie Jones," Rollie said.

"Jay Danvers," the man replied. "Miss Anya Steadman is in here." He guided Rollie into the living room where an elderly woman anxiously sat.

Rollie studied the woman trying to get a sense of who she was. He guessed that she was around eighty or eighty-five years old. She wore her silver hair in a braid wrapped around her head like a crown and her blue eyes looked out of a face creased with few lines. She was slender and somewhat frail but she radiated a strength that belied her years. She could be physically defeated, but she wouldn't submit to Darkness.

"Miss Steadman?" Rollie asked extending his hand in greeting. "I'm Rollie Jones. I'm a representative from the Butler Knights. I've come to take you to where you'll be safe."

The woman shook Rollie's hand, studying his face in turn. She'd been determining people's intentions for so long it was almost automatic. She felt that this young man was one to be trusted, but she'd been wrong before. "Why should I trust you?" she asked.

"You probably shouldn't" Rollie said. "Caution is a survival instinct. But, you know that those who are hunting you are close to finding you and you also know they won't show you any mercy. It's a question of risks. You need to decide if you will take the risk to come with me to possible safety, or to risk running again and most likely be captured. But, we don't have much time for you to decide. Moments only. What do you want to do?"

The woman was silent, considering Rollie's words when the front door opened and Umar came in.

"They're here," he said. "A car just parked up the street. We must leave now."

Rollie held out his hand to the woman and she took it.

"Let's go," Rollie said, helping Miss Steadman to stand, put on her coat and walk to the door. Jay had already left, leaving only the three of them. They hurried to the car Umar had rented at the airport and climbed inside.

"Buckle up," Umar said, revving the engine before putting the car into drive. He peeled away from the curb and shot past a large, black sedan that quickly made a u-turn and began to chase them. Weaving in an out of traffic, he raced down the streets of Boston trying to lose the sedan.

"Their driver is very good," he commented. "Let's try something else."

He barreled along Interstate 90, past Fenway Park then moved into the Back Bay area. He finally spotted what he'd been looking for, a hotel with a parking garage entrance facing the street. The car tires squealed as he made a sudden turn into the garage and pulled to a stop next to a set of double doors leading directly into the lobby.

"Out," he commanded. "Get to the airport. Don't wait for me."

Rollie pulled Miss Steadman out of the car and helped her to run into the hotel. Umar drove further into the garage, attempting to draw their hunters after him. Rollie slowed to a walk as they passed the hotel registration desk and looked out the lobby windows, praying that there was a taxi available. There was. Rollie took a firmer hold on Miss Steadman's arm and calmly walked out the front entrance and opened the taxi's door.

"Boston Harbor Seaplane Base, please," Rollie said to the taxi driver.

"Right," the driver said, setting the meter. They pulled away from the lobby entrance and merged with the traffic. Rollie forced himself to relax and make normal conversation with Miss Steadman to keep her from asking questions. It would be better for the taxi driver to think that they were simple tourists.

"So, Aunt Anya," he began, hoping she'd catch onto his ploy to remain unremarked. "What did you think of Boston?"

"Oh, it was marvelous," she responded. She tightened her hand in his to indicate she understood. "I hope we'll be able to come again. There were so many sights we didn't get to visit." So they passed the time it took to drive to the seaplane base discussing some of the more famous places in Boston. Finally, they arrived. Rollie paid the fare and assisted Miss Steadman out. She looked around and gasped. Striding toward them was Umar Kambuto.

"How did he get here ahead of us?" she asked.

"He has his ways," Rollie said, but wondered the same thing himself.

"We need to hurry," Umar said. "I have the tickets for the next shuttle to New York. It leaves within the hour."

They entered the building and Rollie grabbed a wheelchair for Miss Steadman. "I know I'm old," she said. "But do you really think I need one of these? I thought I'd kept up rather well, under the circumstances."

"It'll help us get through security faster," Rollie said. "I wouldn't normally take advantage, but wheelchairs get priority and we need all the speed we can get."

Both Rollie and Umar were tense as they hurried through the terminal, watching each person, watching for an attack.

"Do you sense anything?" Rollie asked Umar, panting slightly from both the physical and emotional efforts he was employing.

"No, but that can change in a heartbeat," Umar said. "We can't let our guard down for an instance."

Rollie nodded. He wheeled the chair he had Miss Steadman in close to the departure gate and stood next to her. Umar stood slightly in front of them, his presence itself a barrier. His Knight ring glowed ready to defend the woman.

Rollie noticed Miss Steadman shudder and placed his hand on her shoulder. "Try not to worry," he said. "Everything's going to be okay."

Miss Steadman's mouth was pinched and her eyes were filled with fear.

"You don't need to tell me any comforting lies," she said. "I've been running from these evil people since long before you were born. I know very well what will happen if they get their hands on me."

Before Rollie could say anything, their flight was announced. Takeoff was smooth but Rollie saw the woman's hands clench so tightly her knucklebones showed whitely under the skin.

Rollie considered using a spell of calming but changed his mind. He lacked confidence in spell casting and being airborne wasn't the place to have one fizzle out. Besides, she had every right to be terrified and if he was truthful, he was just as frightened. He'd never faced an emissary of the Dark before. Instead, he took several breaths to steady himself and began to speak to her with all of the reassurance he could project. "Try to relax," he said. "We're out of their reach now."

"But, you do know that they'll be looking for me in New York," Miss Steadman said.

"Of course," Rollie said. "But, that's why Umar and I are with you. It's our job to get you to the ship. Once we get aboard, no one and nothing can get at you. The Ladies will see to that."

"Who are these ladies you keep referring to?" Miss Steadman asked.

"We do not discuss them outside of our circle," Umar said. No trace of emotion showed on his face. Miss Steadman felt a chill. Here was someone she wouldn't care to cross.

"Let's just say that they're our employers," Rollie said, trying to project some positivity to counter Umar's stiffness. "You'll like them."

Miss Steadman didn't reply. Instead, she watched out the window. Night had deepened and from the aircraft's vantage, the lights of each town beneath them glowed orange. She used their passing to mark time. So many slipped behind them, how many to go? Finally, the towers that marked the New York skyline came into view. They'd be landing soon. Then what?

Umar took the lead followed by Miss Steadman and then Rollie as they exited the taxi that had driven them to the pier. The outline of the Happenstance appeared ghostly in the fog.

"They're here," Umar said.

"Where?" Rollie asked.

"Ahead on the left," Umar replied.

Rollie felt his breath catch as a wave of cold engulfed them and the fog took on an almost slimy feel. At first, he couldn't see anything then four dark, hazy figures appeared as if conjured out of one of Agnes' steaming caldrons. Their shapes shifted from moment to moment, first human then animal, their eyes glowing yellow. It was difficult to watch them directly.

"What'll we do?" Rollie asked, his voice quavering.

"I'll distract and you make for the ship," Umar said. "Don't stop for anything."

"Right," Rollie said. "On three?"

"Three!" Umar shouted and ran at the figures.

The ship was at least one hundred yards away. The elderly woman wouldn't be able to keep up a running pace long enough to reach it. Rollie made a surprise move and lifted Miss Steadman over his shoulder, then took off running.

In the fog, the pier seemed to keep stretching out before him. Halfway to the ship, his breath became ragged. He focused on putting one foot in front of the next, but his speed was slowing.

"Put me down, Rollie," Miss Steadman said. "You'll never make it carrying me."

"She's right," the warm voice of Miguel Vargas said. He stepped around the light pole that had concealed his presence. "Let me help. There are forces in play tonight."

"Miguel!" Rollie gasped, setting Miss Steadman down. "We have four Dark Hunters on our tail. Umar went after them."

"Umar can take care of himself," Miguel said. "We need to get to the ship. Con permiso, Senora." He took hold of one of her arms while Rollie took the other and they headed down the pier at the fastest pace Miss Steadman could manage, but it was tough going. The further along they traveled, the more difficult each step became. The fog had taken on a sickly, yellow hue and almost seemed to grab at their ankles.

"This isn't normal," Rollie said.

"No," Miguel said. "The fog has been enchanted to work against us and make it easier for the Dark Hunters to catch us."

"Shouldn't our rings protect us?" Rollie asked.

"They should, but for some reason, they are being blocked," Miguel said. "Look at yours."

Rollie looked at his ring. There should have been a green fire flashing deep in the center of the stone. Instead, the stone was muted. "What could do that?" he asked.

"Nothing good," Miguel said.

"Rollie, I can't go any further," Miss Steadman said. She was leaning heavily against Rollie's shoulder and would have slid down to lie in a heap if he hadn't held her up.

"Not to worry," Rollie said, attempting to reassure her. "We're not very far from the ship. We'll get there."

"I hope so," she said. "I'm about done in."

The men again took her arms and began to move, this time at a slow walk. Each step felt as if they were shackled to weights. From behind them, they heard footsteps, coming fast.

"We've got to try and run," Rollie said, taking a more secure hold on Miss Steadman's arm. They took one step and stopped dead. It was as if they had run into a wall. The fog had built up into an almost solid curtain.

"Angamiza!" a voice commanded out of the night and a bright, green flame descended on the fog, evaporating it. Immediately, the dragging sensation left them and they began to run.

"Umar!" Rollie wheezed. Miguel didn't say anything, concentrating on keeping the now staggering woman on her feet. The gangplank leading onto the Happenstance was in sight, but the footsteps were still following them.

Arriving at the foot of the gangplank, Rollie somehow found breath to call out. "Ahoy, Happenstance," he yelled. "Permission to come aboard?"

"Permission granted," came the response. Rollie had only heard that otherworldly voice a few times before since joining the crew and he found it unnerving. He'd been told that it had taken the combined powers of the three Butler sisters to invoke 'The Warder'. Only members of the ship's company and invited guests were permitted aboard. Any intruder was either rebuffed, or otherwise dealt with. Rollie didn't want to think about what that meant. It was a good thing that the Ladies were dedicated to the Power of Light.

The three stepped off the gangplank and almost collapsed onto the deck of the Happenstance. Standing in front of them were Captain Nolan, First Officer Pierce and Agnes Butler.

All three were swathed in heavy coats and knit hats to keep out the night's damp chill. Rollie saw that Miss Steadman's hair was wet and plastered to her head and her teeth were chattering. She needed to get into the warmth of the ship's interior.

"Well done, Mr. Jones," Captain Nolan said then turned to the woman. "Welcome aboard, madam. I'm Captain Nolan. This is Mr. Pierce, our First Officer."

Before he could say anything else, the voice of the Warder boomed out "Permission Denied!" There followed another sound like a massive engine backfire that shook the ship. "Boarding party repelled," the voice intoned.

Rollie looked over the railing. He thought he saw a form crawling away into the darkness but couldn't be sure. He turned back to the people surrounding him and the woman he still held onto.

"Miss Anya Steadman," he said. "May I introduce Miss Agnes Butler?"

Agnes had been studying the other woman and reached out to take her ice-cold hands. "Introductions can wait," she said. "Let's get inside and get you dry and warm." She wrapped her arm around Anya's shoulders and turned them both away from the ship's railing then walked aft to where a set of double doors opened into the lounge.

Rollie's duty aboard was as the ship's steward. That meant he was responsible for the passengers' comfort. He should be with Miss Steadman, seeing to her needs. But, the captain needed to know about Umar. "Captain," he said. "Umar left Miss Steadman in my care and went to deal with a group of four Dark Hunters. We were being chased and the fog had been spelled to slow us down. I'm sure I heard Umar's voice issue an enchantment and the fog lifted, but I didn't see him. Permission to go and look for him?"

"Permission denied," Captain Nolan said.

"But, sir!" Rollie said. "He may need help."

"Mr. Kambuto is one of our best Knights," the captain said. "He knows the risks and how to deal with them. Attend to ship's duties, Mr. Jones. Prepare to get underway, Mr. Pierce. I'll be on the bridge."

"Aye, sir," the first offer said. "Raise the gangplank," he told a seaman standing at the railing. He pulled a small radio out of a pocket and spoke into it as the throb of the ship's engines vibrated through the deck. "Cast off fore and aft lines."

A flurry of activity answered his orders as the ship prepared to set sail. Rollie grabbed the railing and looked back down the pier, hoping to see the image of Umar appear.

Seeing the frown on Rollie's face, Miguel Vargas clapped a hand on his shoulder. "Don't worry about Umar. You've never seen him in action. He's more than a match for just four Dark Hunters. And, if he didn't come aboard, he found something else he needed to do."

"But, he was my partner on this mission and we're leaving him behind," Rollie said. "I should stay and look for him."

"He'll find us," Mr. Pierce said. "And, you need to attend to your ship's duties as the captain ordered. You've a passenger to take care of."

"Si, amigo," Miguel said. "You don't want Miss Agnes to think she made a mistake in choosing you, do you?"

Rollie sighed. He most certainly didn't want any of the Ladies to think he wasn't right for his role as either the ship's steward or as a Knight, especially as a Knight. He turned and followed the women into the lounge where his 'Damsel in Distress' waited.

Chapter Seven: The Baron

It was almost dawn before Anya finally fell asleep and Agnes felt it was safe to leave her. Agnes made her way to the dining room where a coffee service waited.

"Blessed be Cook," she sighed, pouring a steaming cup. Sofie came in a moment later and sat down across from Agnes. She looked at Agnes's eyes, red from lack of sleep.

"It was quite a long night," Sofie said. "Did she say much after you took her to her cabin?"

"Not really," Agnes said. "She told me about how Rollie and Umar saved her. She wanted me to know that Rollie was especially brave and deserved a promotion. I didn't try to explain how the Knight teams actually work, just let her talk. It seemed to help calm her. That, and the draft you put in her tea."

"That reminds me," Sofie said. "You'll need to brew more of the sleeping potion. We used most of what we had retrieving Duval's orb. We've never had to use so much. Not to mention the amount of wine those guards guzzled."

"Alcohol dampens the effect," Agnes said. "But, we were able to retrieve the orb and get it back to Duval. I do wish that so many focus pieces weren't jewelry. It makes them too tempting."

"True," Sofie said. "So, what about Miss Steadman?"

"Well, she's obviously been on the run for a long, long time," Agnes said. "We'll need to gain her trust before she'll open up enough for us to help her."

"We should have Rollie keep close by her," Sofie said. "They've formed a connection and that will help."

"Has Caroline made a prediction? Agnes asked.

"That's what I came to tell you," Sofie said. "She's casting the runes."

"She was reading the Tarot cards last night when we brought Miss Steadman into the lounge," Agnes said. "She waved me off when I tried to introduce Miss Steadman to her. I wonder what she saw that made her toss the bones?"

"She's made three casts," Sofie said. "Once after she read the cards. Again at midnight and just now as the sun rose."

"That's never a good sign," Agnes said. "We'd best go and find out what's worrying her."

The two of them walked back to the lounge where Caroline sat at the same table she'd been at last night. A light hanging over her made the irregularly shaped bone pieces shine. The black symbols etched into them almost seemed to move.

"Caroline?" Agnes asked. "What have you seen?"

"Evil," Caroline said, rising terrified eyes to look at her sisters. "Evil for this Guardian, evil for our Knights and for us. And, if we cannot stop it, evil for the world."

"We've faced evil before," Sofie said. "How is this time different?"

"This Guardian that we rescued has abandoned her trust," Caroline said.

"What?" Sofie asked, astonishment widening her grey eyes. "You mean it was taken from her?"

"No, she chose to leave it," Caroline said.

"How could she do such a thing?" Sofie asked.

"There must be more to it than simple abandonment," Agnes said. "You know that a focus of power never willingly leaves its Guardian except to go to a Wielder."

"There is more," Caroline said. "There is a Wielder. She is a young woman and she is without knowledge of her abilities or of the focus that should come to her."

"Well," Agnes said. "A focus item without a Guardian and an innocent Wielder is about as bad as it can get. She could be twisted by the Dark so easily."

"Sisters," Caroline said. "The danger is greater than anything we've ever faced. The Baron has returned."

"Oh, Great Power of Light, protect us," Agnes said, grabbing the back of a chair to support her sagging legs.

"The Baron?" Sofie asked. "Caroline, are you absolutely certain?"

"Yes," Caroline said. "I saw the trail of blood leading directly to him. He has escaped his prison. His Dark Hunters seek this Guardian and now he knows that we have her. He wants the focus, the Wielder and he wants us. He wants revenge for our family's role in restoring the occult objects stolen by the Nazis. He has found a man who had been one with those criminals and who remains of their mind set. And, he wants revenge for our parents sending him into the prison of Nothingness."

"Nazis?" Captain Nolan asked. The women had been so focused on Caroline that they hadn't noticed him come in. "Are you saying that we're going up against some Nazis?"

"Not just Nazis," Agnes said. "The Baron."

"Who's the Baron?" he asked.

"He's a prime emissary of the Dark Powers," Sofie said. "No one knows where he came from, but stories about his monstrous acts go back centuries."

"Centuries?" Nolan asked somewhat skeptical. "How is that possible?"

"He seeks out objects of power and murders their Wielders most gruesomely to release their powers into the focuses, then drains the power," Agnes said. "This vile practice has extended his life far beyond human mortality. He finds those with darkened minds and hearts and offers them his aid. Most already had plans of greed or vengeance and these plans often involve those dealing with the arcane. They believe that they should have been gifted with powers and were somehow cheated. The Baron convinces these deluded people that he is the only one who can help them achieve success and gain their desires. But he demands that they share power with him. When they agree, as so many have done, he makes their plans come to fruition. But, this lasts only for a short time. Then, things fall apart leaving only death as a way out for his stooges."

"Horrible," Nolan said, at a loss for more words.

"You see his influence in the bloody stories recorded in history books," Agnes said. "He's only been caught once. His own greed tripped him up and it resulted in his being banished into another existence, a magical prison, for want of a better description. But, his capture cost us most dearly. It was paid for by the deaths of our grandparents and sent our parents into a hermit's existence."

"How did he escape?" Nolan asked.

"That we don't know," Caroline said. "Years after the war, our parents and grandparents were attempting to locate objects of the occult that were stolen from their Wielders or Guardians by the Nazis. It was like what happened with the great artworks from all over Europe."

"Our family's mission was to retrieve these objects and restore them to their proper Wielders or Guardians," Sofie said. "Barring that they were to keep the objects safe until new Wielders could be found. They were having some success when The Baron tried to pervert them and gather the objects for himself."

"Our mother and grandmother combined their powers to halt The Baron while our father and grandfather transported a number of the objects to safety," Sofie said. "Centuries of devouring power made The Baron immensely strong. It was only when the men returned that they were able to cast The Baron into Nothingness and seal the door. You see our father had brought the Rod of Compassion with him. But, even with the Rod's power, the effort drained the four of them."

"It killed our grandparents and almost our parents, too," Agnes said. "Over time, our parents regained their powers, but to this day, they refuse to acknowledge it."

"So, that's when you ladies took up the task." Nolan said.

"Not immediately," Sofie said. "We were quite young and still in our training. We had an idea that we might continue their quest but it wasn't until Caroline had the vision that we knew what we were supposed to do. You know the rest."

"So, somehow this Baron has escaped from prison and is hungry for power," Nolan said. "If he is running true to form, he's found a stooge to work on and they're now looking for our guest and her focus object."

"I believe you're correct, Captain," Agnes said.

"I know that you ladies don't like to pry into our rescues' lives under the Powers, but this involves the safety of the ship," he said. "I'm sorry but I must insist that we get all of the information about who Miss Steadman is and what her focus does before we reach London. It was no secret that we were leaving New York heading for London. The Baron could have an entire army of Dark Hunters waiting for us and even the whole circle's combined powers may not be enough to hold them off. We'll need a plan to deal with them."

"Captain Nolan," Sofie said. "Your concern does you credit, but-"

"But," he interrupted. "I have worked for and with you ladies for three years. I've seen you do things that would make normal people think they've gone stark raving mad and you're the good guys. From what you just told me, this Baron may well be beyond your scope. You said that I have a bit of a gift. Well, if I do, it's telling me that we must have a plan and that means we must have information."

"Captain Nolan is correct," Caroline said. "I keep hearing the name Anna. Not Anya, but Anna. It is Anna is at the heart of The Baron's quest. We must know about her and Miss Steadman has that knowledge."

"We're strangers to her," Agnes said. "She isn't going to trust us with her most precious information."

"The innocent Wielder," Caroline said. "She will risk everything to protect the one the focus is to go to. We must make her understand the danger that awaits."

"Do you see a way?" Nolan asked.

"Rollie," Caroline said, echoing Sofie's earlier comment. "He'll be able to extract what's needed to retrieve the focus object and protect the Wielder."

"Well, let's get him looped in on this mess and see what he can do to get it straightened out," Agnes said.

Nodding, the captain walked over to an intercom mounted on the wall and pressed a button. "Mr. Jones," the captain's voice echoed through the ship. "Come to the lounge. Mr. Jones to the lounge, please."

Chapter Eight: Remka

Rollie had his instructions from Captain Nolan and the Ladies. It was up to him to win Miss Steadman's trust and get her to talk about the focus she was supposed to be guarding and where she'd left it. Did she understand what she'd done? And finally, who was the Wielder? That was a major load to drop on him and in no way did he feel confident that he'd be able to get the information. Surely one of the Ladies would be much better suited. But, they'd said that a tentative connection had been forged between Miss Steadman and him during the rescue and that would give him an opening.

Rollie stood outside Miss Steadman's cabin trying to think of how he'd approach her, but his mind was a complete blank. "Stupid," he said to himself. He was supposed to be the extraction expert, wasn't he? So, get on with it.

Rollie knocked on the door and announced himself. "Room steward, Miss Steadman," he said, listening for her response.

"Come in, Rollie," she said.

He opened the door and entered. "Good morning," he said, smiling at the woman. She had obviously been up for awhile. She was dressed in the clothing the Ladies had left and her hair was neatly styled.

"Good morning," she said, smiling. "Do I thank you for the clean clothes?"

"That would be Miss Agnes," he said. "Would you like to have breakfast now? I can bring it to you or you are welcome to come to the dining room."

"Oh, I don't want to be a bother to you," she said.

"Not at all," he said. "I'm here to look after your comfort while you're aboard the Happenstance."

"Thank you," she said. "I'll go to the dining room, if you'll show me the way."

Rollie smiled at her and walked her to the dining room. He seated her at one of the smaller tables near a large window where she could look out at the ocean. It was an overcast day and the water reflected the grey clouds, so the view wasn't inspiring, but it gave the impression of openness.

"Breakfast today is either ham, eggs and toast or quiche with fruit cup," he said. "We also have coffee, tea and juice."

"I'd like some coffee, please," she said.

"Certainly," he said and he went to get her a cup.

"Delicious," she said after taking a sip.

"Miss Agnes is a bit of a snob when it comes to coffee," Rollie said. "But don't tell her I said so."

She chuckled and gave him her meal selection. She looked out at the rolling water while he went to the galley. He returned a few minutes later and sat a plate with a slice of quiche and a cup of fruit in front of her then refilled her coffee cup.

"Would you like anything else?" he asked.

"Have you eaten?" she asked in return.

"Yes," he said.

"Well, would you get into trouble if I asked you to sit with me?" she asked. "I've never enjoyed eating by myself if I had a choice and I've been alone for a long time."

"No, I won't get into trouble," he said slipping into the chair across from her. "And I'd enjoy talking with you."

"Am I permitted to ask questions?" she asked.

"You're not a prisoner, Miss Steadman," he said. "You're our guest. I admit that we sort of forced you to come with us, but I'm sure you'll agree that the alternative wasn't one you wanted to face. You're free to leave the ship anytime. Well, anytime after we get into port. Or, you may want to remain under the Butler Knights' protection."

"Who exactly are the Butler Knights?" she asked. "In fact, who are the Butler Ladies? I don't mean superficial introductions, I mean what are they?"

Rollie studied her face, considering how to explain. He decided that only the truth would work, so he told her the story of how the three sisters had received a sending to use their powers to help others threatened by dark forces. How they'd determined that using a tramp freighter would give them unobtrusive access to ports all over the world and be a base from which they could dispatch Knight teams.

"But knights of what kingdom?" she asked.

Rollie chuckled. "The name started out as a bit of a joke," he said. "One of the sisters, Miss Caroline, compared the people they'd chosen to be rescuers to the knights from fairytales who were sent on quests and rescued fair maidens from fire breathing dragons. Over time, it became habit to refer to the team members as knights. Specifically, Butler Knights in honor of the Ladies."

"So, I ask again," she said. "Who are these ladies?"

"They're Wielders of the Powers of Light," he said. "In other words, they're witches."

"I suspected that might be the case," she said. "I felt something when Agnes took my hands last night. I never had the opportunity to learn from my mother. She was one with great power. How often I've wished that I could've learned from her."

"How did she die?" he asked.

"She didn't die," she said. "She left."

"She abandoned you?" he asked. "That doesn't sound like an act of a Wielder of Light."

"She didn't abandon me and my brother," she said. "I said she left, but I should have said that she was taken. She was taken by Remka."

"Who is Remka, if I might ask?" Rollie asked. He had a feeling that she was about to tell him what he needed without any intrigue on his part.

"You put your life at risk to save mine," she said. "Your friend Umar may have died because of me. I guess I owe you an explanation, at least."

"No," Rollie said. "Tell me only if it's what you want to do, not because you feel an obligation. There is no obligation to me or to Umar. We chose to come to your aid because it was the right thing to do, not for any reward or imagined quid pro quo."

Miss Steadman was silent, thinking. She felt a longing to confide in someone. It had been so long since she'd been able to do that. Even her brother, George, had rebuffed her when she tried to talk about their mother. And, she'd never told William, her late husband, about who and what her family was. He wouldn't have believed her. But, here was someone who would understand. Yes, she would tell Rollie all about her family and about Remka. Young as she had been, she remembered all she'd been told about Remka and her Light.

"Perhaps we could find somewhere less public where I can tell you the story," she said.

"I assure you that everyone aboard is trustworthy or they wouldn't be here, Miss Steadman," he said, smiling. "But, if you'd feel better, we could go back to your cabin."

"Thank you, Rollie," she said. "As I am taking the liberty of calling you by your given name, please call me Anya."

Rollie stood up and held the chair for Anya. They returned to her cabin and he saw that she was comfortable in one of the two, deeply cushioned chairs that formed a sitting area across from the bed. He took the other and waited for her to begin her story.

"I must go far back in history to begin this tale," she said. "To the early 1600's. I'm sure that you've heard about the Thirty Years War."

Rollie nodded. "Most of Europe was involved," he said.

"Yes," Anya said. "By some accounts, upwards of half the population was killed before it ended in 1648. There was a man called Peter who somehow survived. Weary of fighting and death, he took what few remained of his family and neighbors and led them on a journey to find a new home. They must have been desperate to follow him into the unknown. They had little in the way of possessions and livestock, but they gathered what they could and headed into the wilderness that was the Alps.

"Desperation is a powerful motivator," Rollie said. "Look at how today's wars and famines make so many thousands of people emigrate to other countries in an effort to find safety."

"Peter was an astute leader," Anya said. "He seemed to have an insight about where they were to go. Perhaps he'd been in the area they traveled during the war. Or, maybe he'd received a vision. However it happened, he led his people for weeks, up and down boulder-strewn mountain passes and across glacier fed streams until finally, almost at the end of their strength, they came through a deep, dark gorge that opened into a wide, shallow valley at the base of a tall mountain. Here, the sun was warm and the grass was deep and green."

"It must have seemed like a paradise," Rollie said.

Anya smiled, a far away look in her eyes. "It was," she said. "But to continue, Peter declared that they would make the valley their new home and he named it 'Das Bergtal Freiheit', Freedom Valley. Over time, they and their descendants built a small village they called 'Freiheit Dorf' or Freedom Village where they lived peacefully for over one hundred years. Then came Napoleon and another war. His armies ranged all over central Europe, Russia and into Egypt and Syria. The village began to see more travelers passing through. Some were military couriers and others, like their ancestors, were those seeking asylum. Unfortunately, they also brought diseases that the villagers in their isolation had no immunity to. One was a fever that struck the children particularly hard."

Rollie nodded his head. "Like the polio virus," he said.

"One night, a woman walked into the village all alone," Anya said. "She was small of stature, brown skinned with black hair and eyes, wrapped in tatters, her feet bare. She stood in the middle of the village and called out.

'I have traveled over deserts, across seas and mountains to find this village,' she said. 'I know that your children are ill. By your leave, I offer healing.'

" Most of the villagers were afraid of her and barred their doors. But, in spite of her strange appearance, the headman had her brought into his house. His little daughter was gravely ill and he feared that she wouldn't live through the night. He asked the woman if she could truly heal his child and how much she wanted as they had little to pay for such.

"She looked at the girl and said that she had the skill to cure her and would endeavor to do so. She did not want gold. Instead, she asked to live in the village without anyone from the outside world knowing that she did. The headman became suspicious demanded to know from what she was fleeing. She replied that her only crime was one of being different."

"Given how you described her she would have stuck out among a population of mostly fair complexioned people," Rollie said. "Fear of her wouldn't be unexpected for those times."

"Before he could say anything the little girl moaned, her distress growing," Anya said. "The headman felt he had no choice but to agree to the woman's terms. She immediately brewed a potion from herbs she carried in a bag and dosed the child, putting her into a deep sleep. She pulled an amulet from around her neck, holding it in her right hand and she placed her left hand on the child's forehead. A blue stone in the middle of the amulet began to glow and a light such as the headman had never seen traveled up the woman's arm, across her breast and down the other, enveloping the child's head. It's unknown how long the woman fed this power to the child, but in the end, the fever broke and the girl recovered. The headman told the other villagers of his daughter's miracle cure and of his agreement to house and hide the woman. Others asked if the woman would consent to heal their children. She agreed and cured them as she had the headman's daughter.

"The villagers, while grateful, were still distrustful of this strange women. Some wanted the headman to send her away. But, the headman refused. He'd given his word that she could live with them and that they would keep her presence secret. However, he realized that part of their fear was that they did not yet know her or what she intended to do. He went to where she had erected a small tent and sat with her.

'How shall we call you, lady?' he'd asked. 'And what do you wish to do among us?'

"The woman looked into his eyes as if to assure herself of his intentions. Finally, she nodded and spoke.

'You may call me Remka,' she said. 'If you will keep my presence secret, as you promised, I will care for your people and bring the blessings of the Light to your village.'

'So be it,' the headman said.

"He was an honorable man," Rollie said. "It wouldn't have been surprising if he'd sent her away."

"Yes, he was true to his word," Anya said. "He had the villagers build Remka a hut at the edge of the village and provided her with food, clothing and other necessities. She took a young girl orphaned by the fever into her hut and began to teach her the healing ways. The child's name was Anya and she was my ancestor.

"Anya learned much more than healing, for Remka was a mystic and a woman of power. The village prospered under Remka's care and as the years passed, some of the villagers forgot their promise of silence and bragged about their wise woman."

"Human nature," Rollie said. "Some people just can't keep secrets."

Anya nodded her head in agreement. "Although still isolated, the village was no longer unknown to the outside world," she said. "Roads had been built and traders often came. It was from these traders that word of the village's wise woman reached a powerful merchant in another township. He determined that he would take the woman and use her to increase his fortune.

"On the last full moon of summer, the village was startled by a blue light so bright that it could be seen inside of the houses shuttered for the night. The light came from the base of the mountain behind the village. Alarmed, the village men ran to see what it was. But, as suddenly as it had appeared, it died away. Then, a sound of bells clanging broke the night's stillness. Echoing back and forth across the valley, the sound all but deafened the villagers.

"When the clamor faded, a lone figure walked the path from the mountain back to the village. It was Anya and around her neck was the amulet Remka always wore. She stopped when she reached the men.

'Where is Remka?' the men asked.

'She has gone on,' Anya replied.

'Where has she gone?' the headman asked. 'Why has she left us?'

'She is a woman of great power and has gone to another realm where her power will be welcomed,' Anya said. 'As to why, those who forgot their promise of silence have brought our village to the attention of a very evil man. Remka foresaw he would bring death to our people if she remained. Death may still be our portion. This evil one craves Remka's power as one parched by heavy labor craves cool water. His evil is beyond Remka's teachings but he would take what she gave to me and leave our people with nothing but pain and despair. Therefore, I will go to the high meadows to gather herbs until he leaves or death comes for us. It will be your burden to thwart him.'

"And so it happened. The evil merchant did come and brought many savage and brutal men with him. The villagers had hoped to trick the merchant into believing that Remka had died. They'd made a grave and carved a headstone. The merchant did not wish to believe and had houses searched, villagers beaten. Those who were questioned by the evil one soon broke and told him that Remka had made magic that took her to another world. Upon hearing this, the evil merchant made them show him where she'd performed her spell. He stalked back and forth seeking some sign, often lifting his head and sniffing the air as if he could smell her presence."

"That must have been so terrifying for those villagers," Rollie said.

"Yes," Anya said. "They were a simple people, unused to such treatment." She paused for a moment, thinking of the defenseless people faced with such a situation. Rollie remained silent as he waited for her to finish her story.

"Eventually, the evil merchant and his men left the village," she said. "Anya returned but refused to use the amulet Remka had given her. She taught her daughter as Remka had taught her so that the healing and protective wisdom wouldn't be lost, but forbade the use of the amulet unless there was grave danger to the village."

Chapter Nine: Anya

Anya paused her story again and Rollie went to get her a drink of water. "Would you like to rest?" he asked. "We can continue later."

"No," Anya said. "I've started telling this story and somehow, I must continue. I know that there's a great deal of danger and someone needs to know what I have never told anyone else."

"As you wish," Rollie said. "But, let me know when you tire."

"Of course," Anya said. She sat silent for a few more moments, gathering her thoughts. Rollie sat quietly. He understood that this was the information they needed and his job was to listen as carefully as possible.

"As time passed, Anya married and her daughter in turn took guardianship of the amulet," Anya said. "And so it continued, generation after generation, the amulet passed from mother to daughter. Then, in the late 1930's, evil again came. World War II broke out. Switzerland was neutral, but there was a plan by the Nazis to invade. One night, in 1943, my mother had a vision and awoke screaming. The village was going to be taken over, the townspeople murdered and replaced by Nazi troops. Their only escape was to follow Remka into a far, mystic realm. In her vision, Remka had called to my mother and told her how to use the amulet to open the portal so that the village could escape. But, time was short. They must leave immediately and there could be no return. Anyone left behind would face certain death.

"My mother's fear was convincing, so the villagers gathered what they could and rushed to the base of the mountain behind the village. There, my mother, brother and I waited. When all were gathered, mother took the amulet from her neck and off the chain. She breathed on it then, on a flat stone, she set it spinning.

"Wisps of blue light began to gather and swirl around. It grew brighter and brighter until the entire mountainside was illuminated. Then, my mother made a motion with her hands and the blue light swept into the mountain. A shimmer developed and a sort of tunnel became visible. On the other side, a green meadow appeared. Walking across it was a dark haired, brown skinned woman. It was Remka. She beckoned the people to come to her, but most of them were too terrified to move.

'Go to her,' my mother commanded. Timidly, one man stepped forward and stepped across to the other side. Then, the rest of the people followed.

"I was only four years old at the time. My mother was so concerned with saving the village that we'd left our house without packing anything. I suddenly remembered that I'd left my doll at our home. I couldn't let the bad men get her so I broke away and ran to retrieve her. I heard my mother cry out for me to come back and then my older brother, George say he'd get me. He ran after me and caught me by the arm. We turned back, but it was too late. We saw our mother lifted up and sucked through the tunnel. The green meadow darkened and the shimmer stopped. The blue light grew and grew until we had to shield our eyes, then it died away. We ran back and my brother called out for mother to come back, but the only sound was a clink as the spinning amulet fell over on the rock.

"I bent over and picked up the amulet. I felt a warm tingle run through my hand. That's when the sound of bells began to ring. Louder and louder the sound became. It echoed all around us, so painful that we had to cover our ears with our hands. Then, the ringing stopped.

But a terrible shaking and a roar that was the sound of half the mountainside falling on top of our village immediately replaced it. Nothing was left. To this day, I don't know how George and I were spared. We should have been crushed, entombed with the village I can only surmise that the amulet protected us.

"We wandered along the road until we were found by one of the Swiss army patrols. Eventually, we were sent to live with a family in Bern. I was eighteen when George married and immigrated to the United States. As he was all the family I had, I went with him. A few years later, a man arrived from Germany. He introduced himself as Herr Vogel and he told us that he'd been a scout for a Swiss patrol during the war and had witnessed a miracle. He'd seen our mother open the portal and our village escape into the mystic land. He'd witnessed the destruction of our village, but was caught and injured by a rock fall. He'd spent many years tracking us down. He knew that our mother had used an enchanted amulet to open the portal, and he offered to buy it. He said he hoped that the enchantment could provide another miracle and cure his paralysis.

"My brother scoffed at the idea of a portal or an enchanted amulet. He'd made himself believe that our village had been buried in a landslide and all of the people, except us, killed. The amulet was just a piece of old jewelry and he was willing to sell it, if the price was right. He judged that the man was quite wealthy and could afford to pay a considerable amount.

"I, on the other hand, did not trust the man. He was German, but said he'd been a part of the Swiss military. He said he'd seen our mother open the portal, but not why he'd been spying on the village. If he'd been there legitimately, he'd have sought shelter in the village for the night. Furthermore, the amulet was telling me not to trust him. You see, as my mother had done, I now wore Remka's Light out of sight around my neck and it had grown icy cold and little, sharp shocks flicked my skin. And, I seemed to see two images of Herr Vogel, one on top of the other. One was the congenial, smiling man who was looking for a miracle. The other was one infected with an evil madness. Of him, I was afraid.

"My brother urged me to sell the amulet, but I refused. I said that it was all I had of mother's and that to me it was priceless. Herr Vogel became very angry and began to shout threats at me. I became more frightened and ran out of the room. Somehow, I knew that my life would be at risk if I remained where he could find me, so during the night I left."

Anya paused to take a sip of water and sat, lost in her thoughts. Rollie sat, almost afraid to move. Finally, Anya sighed and began to speak again.

"I traveled all over the United States, working then moving on," she said. "I felt that I was being followed. I went to Canada and to Mexico and South America, then back. I met my husband, William, when I returned. He was quite wealthy and was able to protect me. I never told him about the amulet. I only said that a crazed man believed that I had brought something of value with me when I came from Switzerland and he wanted it so much that he'd been hunting me. Unfortunately, William passed away far too soon. But he left me with enough wealth that I could keep myself safe.

" Meanwhile, George and his wife had had a son, who in turn also had a son and that son had a daughter. Out of tradition, they named her Anna, in my honor. I attended her Christening and gave her parents a substantial check as a gift. But, her birth gave me what I hoped was a way to safeguard Remka's Light.

"I set up a trust fund for Anna and had a legal firm place the amulet into a bank safe deposit box with instructions that it all be turned over to Anna on her twenty-fifth birthday. With the amulet, I included a letter telling her the same story I just told you. I also asked that she attempt to find me so that we could go back to where the village had been. You see I too want to find out if the portal could be opened and if I could join those who had gone ahead.

"It has been twenty-five years and until recently, I had felt that I was safe. But something's changed. It is almost as if some force knows that it is time for the amulet to reappear. I started noticing strange men around my flat, following me. I was terrified.

"Then, a few nights ago, I had a dream. It was so vivid, like none I've ever had. My mother stood at my bedside, smiling at me and she told me that she still loved me. She said that I was in terrible danger and that the only way to escape was to go to Boston and seek out the Butler Mission office. There I would find help. If I didn't, I would die, Anna would be killed and Remka's Light would become a tool of the Dark. It was my duty to see that none of it happened.

"I woke, immediately dressed and took a train to Boston. I checked into a hotel and used their business center to do an Internet search for Butler Mission. I really wasn't expecting to find anything, but the search returned just the one result. I clicked on the link and what appeared to be a logo appeared. It was a rather whimsical image of a knight's shield crossed by three broomsticks. Below that was an address. That was all.

I closed down the computer and turned to go to my room. That's when I saw a man dressed in black at the registration desk. I just knew that he was asking about me, so I ducked around the corner and went out the back door. I flagged down a taxi and went to the address listed on the website. It was late and I was afraid that the office would be closed, but the young man, Jay, answered my knock. You know the rest."

Anya hugged herself and shivered with a chill born out of exhaustion.

"We have several days before we get to England," Rollie said. "You should rest and get your strength back. You also should think about what you want to do. If you want the help of the Ladies and the Butler Knights, it's yours for the asking. We don't want any focus of the Light to fall into the clutches of the Dark Ones and we'll do everything in our power to prevent it. The teams have done so many times by retrieving focuses and rescuing Wielders and Guardians. We can help you, too, but not without your permission or a direct sending from the Light."

"Thank you, Rollie," Anya said. "I will rest now and I'll think about what to do. Would it be possible to discuss my situation with your Ladies sometime before we dock in England?"

"Absolutely," Rollie said, smiling. "They'd be happy to speak with you. With your permission, I could tell them what you have already told me. That way, they'll be up to speed and have a chance to think about options. May I?"

"I think it would be a good idea," she said.

Rollie stood up to leave, but stopped to take her hand. He held it for a long moment to provide some reassurance then left her to rest.

Chapter Ten: The Crossing

Rollie hurried to the lounge where the Ladies waited. All three looked up as he entered.

"I take it you were able to get her to talk with you?" Agnes asked.

"Yes," he said. "But it was her decision, not anything I did."

"Of course, Rollie," Sofie said. "She needed to talk and you have her trust. That's important because time isn't on our side. We need her to help us."

"She gave me permission to relate her story to you," he said.

Agnes waved him to take the chair opposite the sofa where the three women sat.

Rollie carefully related everything Anya had told him. The Ladies listened without interruption. When he'd finished, they remained silent for several moments.

"Well done, Rollie," Agnes said. "That's much more information than I anticipated getting."

"Remka's Light," Sofie said. Her brow was wrinkled as she tried to think if she'd ever heard of it. "Anya said that Remka had crossed deserts and seas. Based on that, she might have come from India, Asia or somewhere in the Middle East or Africa."

"Is that important?" Rollie asked.

"It could be," Caroline replied. "These regions had advanced sorcery thousands of years ago. As you know, a focus absorbs the Wielder's powers at the time of their deaths. If Remka's Light is one of the ancient focuses, it could well hold an immense amount of power and that makes it a prime target for the Baron."

"Don't even think about it," Agnes said. "If he gets his hands on something that powerful, he'd be practically unstoppable."

"Anya asked to talk with you," Rollie said. "I may have overstepped myself, but I advised her to think about what she wanted to do and if she wanted our help. I didn't tell her what I thought she needed to do."

"Very good, Rollie," Caroline said. "Pushing her might have had the opposite result. She must make her own choice to either accept our help, or continue to run and eventually, be caught."

"And if she chooses to run?" Rollie asked.

"Then she runs," Agnes said. "Of course, we'll follow. Just because someone declines our help doesn't mean we don't still help. It just makes it harder for us to work unseen."

"Right," Rollie said, the gap in his teeth showed as he smiled. He was relieved at Agnes' words. He didn't know what he'd do if Anya refused their help. She was his first real rescue and he felt responsible for her. "So, when would you like to see her?"

"We'll invite her to have dinner with us," Agnes said. "Give her a chance to get to know us and understand what we can offer her and her great grandniece."

"The niece is like Anya," Caroline said. "She has the gift, but not the training. She's never been exposed to the workings of the Power. She's totally innocent. That makes her even more of a prize for the Baron. We must get to her first."

"We will," Agnes said. "We'll have dinner in the situation room, Rollie."

"I'll set it up," he said, standing up. He bowed his head to the Ladies and left the lounge.

Several hours later, Rollie escorted Anya to the situation room. It had been transformed from a basic conference room into a private dining nook. He'd set the table for four using a snowy, white tablecloth and napkins, china, crystal goblets and shining silverware. He'd placed a low centerpiece with four, short candles set in a ring. It gave the table warmth and elegance. Sofie had ordered coq au vin for dinner and a selection of pastries with coffee for desert. "You can't beat French cuisine to bring out pleasant conversation," she'd said.

A few minutes before dinner was ready, Rollie went to fetch Anya.

"Good evening, Anya," Agnes said, taking Anya's hand. "I hope you were able to get some rest."

"Yes, some," Anya said. "And, thank you for your help. I owe you all so much."

"You owe us nothing," Caroline said. "We are servants of the Light. The Light directed you to us."

"Why don't we have our dinner while we get to know one another?" Sofie asked. She motioned the others toward the table and Rollie, who'd been standing nearby, held the chairs for each of the woman, then brought the food.

"I'm surprised to find Women of Power aboard a ship at sea," Anya said. "From what little I know, iron and water should drain your powers. I know they usually make me feel, all weak and fuzzy. But, everything seems perfectly normal."

"It took some doing," Sofie said. "We were fortunate that the ship was in dry dock when we took possession. We were able to cleanse and seal her before we put to sea."

"But, why a ship?" Anya asked.

"The ship provides us with cover," Agnes said. "Who'd think that a tramp freighter, hauling legitimate cargos would also be a fortress from which our knights venture forth on their quests?" She chuckled a bit at her whimsy. "Seriously, we'd be hard put to keep multiple land locations secret from the Dark Ones."

"I see," Anya said. "But, you had an office and a house in Boston."

"Boston and the surrounding towns have a long history of struggles involving the Powers. We keep a contact office there as help is often needed quickly."

"Yes," Anya said. "That makes sense. I remember reading about the Salem witch trials."

The ladies shifted uncomfortably and Sofie made a warding sigh against evil. Noticing the concern on Anya's face, Agnes smiled. "Sorry," she said. "Family history."

"Speaking of family," Sofie said. "What about your great grandniece? Have you thought about what you want to do?"

"I've done nothing but think," Anya said. "In my attempt to protect her, I appear to have put her directly in the path of danger."

Tears spilled down her cheeks and she chocked back a sob. Agnes reached across the table and placed her hand over Anya's. "There, dear," she said. "We're here to help."

"Can you really help me?" Anya asked. "Can you help me protect Anna? I know you sent Rollie and Umar to bring me to the safety of your ship but look what happened. Umar was killed and those Dark Hunters now know about your ship. They'll be waiting for you when you dock in London. I've ruined everything you've built. By rights, you should throw me overboard."

"Are you finished feeling sorry for yourself?" Sofie asked after giving Anya a moment more to cry. "Because you are talking absolute nonsense. In the first place, no one outside of our crew and selected passengers ever sees the Happenstance as anything but an old, tramp freighter. And no one is able to board without getting past the Warder. So far, no one ever has. And a part of our defense includes a memory charm. Those denied boarding have their memories of the ship completely wiped and they are left disoriented.

"As for Umar, well let's just say that there's more to him than you saw and he has his own reasons to have disappeared. I have no doubt but that we'll find him waiting for us in one port or another. Our mission is not ruined. But, we still need to know if you want our help."

Anya had been shocked by Sofie's words. She had, indeed been feeling sorry for herself. But, she looked at the Ladies and then at Rollie and saw encouragement. She felt a small surge of courage.

"All I've ever done is to run away," she said. "I'm too old to continue running. Anna doesn't know me, but I'd give my life to keep her safe. What do you recommend I do?"

Almost as one, the three Ladies nodded their heads in satisfaction.

"First things first," Agnes said. "You're going to get a good night's sleep and then tomorrow, you'll tell us everything you know and remember about your niece, the amulet and your Herr Vogel. Then, we'll decide what resources we'll need."

"Thank you," Anya whispered, tearing up again.

"Rollie," Sofie said. "Why don't you take Anya back to her cabin and bring her some tea or hot chocolate."

"Yes, Miss Sofie," Rollie said, extending his arm to Anya. "You can trust the Ladies and the Butler Knights to help."

Early the next morning Anya awoke with a clear mind. She suspected that there was more than tea in the cup Rollie had brought her last night, but she'd been too tired to care. She showered and dressed, thankful for Agnes's thoughtfulness in providing her with more clean clothes then made her way to the dining room. There, she found the Ladies, Rollie, Captain Nolan, Mr. Pierce and Miguel Vargas waiting for her. The men stood as she entered. The Ladies all smiled.

"Good morning, Miss Steadman," Captain Nolan said. He held the chair for her while Rollie poured coffee. "What would you like for breakfast?"

Anya noticed a stack of dishes on a tray waiting to be taken back to the galley. The others must have risen even earlier than she and had already eaten.

"I'm much too keyed up to be hungry," she said. "Just coffee, for now."

"Very well," Nolan said. "You might be surprised that I am included in this meeting, but as the captain, the welfare of everyone on board is my responsibility. I must know what's being planned and if it impacts the ship or its operations."

"I trust you remember Mr. Pierce and Mr. Vargas," Agnes said, inclining her head at the smiling man sitting next to Miss Caroline.

"Yes, of course," Anya said. "Good morning Mr. Pierce and Mr. Vargas. Thank you for your help the other night, Mr. Vargas"

"Buenos dias, Senora Steadman," Miguel said from across the table. "I was glad to be of assistance. I hope to be at your service in the coming days."

"I think we should get started," Sofie said. "As we said last evening, we'll need all of the information you can provide. Because her life is at risk, we'll start with your niece. Tell us everything you know."

"To begin, her full name is Anna Lynn Steadman," Anya said. "She lives, or at least her family did live in Denver, Colorado and she will turn twenty-five in two weeks. That's when she's to receive the money from the trust fund I set up for her and also when she'll take possession of Remka's Light."

"You don't have her current address?" Miguel asked.

"No," Anya said. "I remember my brother's as I lived with him and his wife for several years, but I don't have hers."

"How is she to be contacted regarding the trust?" Nolan asked.

"The law firm had her parents' address. If that's no longer valid, I'd assume they would find some way to trace her."

The others were quiet, waiting for Anya to continue.

"The last time I saw Anna, she was only a baby. I didn't dare keep in touch for fear Herr Vogel would find and take her. You see, I knew. I knew when I held her that she had power and that the amulet would become hers. But, I needed to stay away until she was ready.

Twenty-five years is a long time. I might not have lived long enough to explain everything to her. So, I put it all into my letter to her."

"She won't believe it," Sofie said. "Who would?"

"I think the amulet will take care of that," Caroline said. "Taking possession of a focus tends to open a mind."

"Speaking of the amulet," Rollie said. "What can you tell us about it? What does it look like? How big is it?"

"Well, it's a bit smaller than my palm, say about an inch and a half in diameter," Anya said. "It's a round, copper bezel holding a copper triangle. In the middle of the triangle is light blue star sapphire. There are etchings around the bezel that might be some kind of writing, runes maybe, but I couldn't read them. It's very old."

"Undoubtedly it's one of the ancient amulets of power," Sofie said. "Great care will have to be taken. Only a Wielder or a Guardian should handle it. Anyone else could be injured."

"There's something else," Anya said. "You'll think that I'm delusional, but..."

"But?" Agnes prompted.

"Remka's Light is somehow alive," Anya said. "It speaks to you. Not speaks with words, but it communicates. It grows warm and it tingles when something is good and it turns cold and stings when there's evil."

"And that's what will convince Anna to believe," Caroline said. "Once she holds it, it will claim her."

"That's what happened to me when I picked it up after my mother was taken," Anya said. "I knew I was supposed to do things with it, but I didn't know what or how."

"You became a Guardian, not a Wielder," Sofie said. "Pity. You would probably have been able to work much good in the world had you the training."

"So, what does this mean for our mission?" Pierce asked.

"Well, we obviously need to locate Anna and have a team on hand when she receives the amulet," Agnes said. "Do you remember the name of the law firm you engaged?"

"Yes," Anya said. "It was Higley and Carter. They were one of the best firms dealing with wills and inheritances, although I expect Mr. Higley senior has passed. Also, the National Bank of the Rockies is where the safe deposit box is located."

"So, a trip to Colorado, find the girl, get her and the amulet safely to where?" Miguel asked.

"Do you still want to return to your old home?" Agnes asked.

"If possible," Anya said. "But I won't ask Anna to do anything she doesn't want to do. Dropping all of this on her is going to be more than enough of a burden. But, 'Freiheit Dorf' still calls to me. It was where I last saw my mother and friends. If the amulet would work and the portal open, I believe that it would need to be there."

"Then the plan is to bring Anna and the amulet to Switzerland?" Rollie asked.

"No," Agnes said. "Milan, I think."

"Agnes!" Sofie said. "You can't mean to bring them into this."

"I do think we need to consult them," Agnes said. "We only have the stories of how they dealt with the Baron. They have the actual experience so will be able to anticipate his possible actions. Besides, the villa would be much more comfortable. And, it will make a good staging area."

"Whom are you talking about?" Nolan asked.

"Our mother and father," Agnes said. "They've been living in Milan, Italy for several years. It's about time they shook off the cobwebs and stopped wasting their talents."

"I know you've never agreed with them on this, but it was their choice to retire," Sofie said. "What makes you think they'd agree to help?

"That's easy," Agnes said. "The Baron. They would do anything if it meant we could get rid of him."

"Excuse me," Anya said. "But, wouldn't it be wiser to keep knowledge of this affair to as few people as possible? You know, 'lose lips sink ships'. I mean no disrespect, but secrecy is how I've stayed ahead of Vogel."

"Anya," Agnes said. "I don't mean to frighten you, but the real danger isn't from Herr Vogel. There is an even greater enemy. It's the Baron. He is a sorcerer of great power and completely evil. You know of him, or I think you do. I believe he was the evil merchant who came to the village. If he gets his hands on you, Anna or the amulet, he'd not only kill you, he'd suck you dry of your powers and with Remka's Light, he'd be on a course for world domination. This has been his intent for at least three centuries. Most of the wars in Europe and the Middle East can be laid to his manipulations. It may well take the efforts of multiple talents to stop him. Possibly multiple lives"

Everyone around the table looked concerned and was thinking what their role would now be in this matter.

"Alright," Nolan said. "We've got another six days until we reach London. Whom do you want on the Knight team? We can spare up to eight men without seriously impacting the ship's operation. More if we stay docked in London. But, I'm assuming you'll want to head to Genoa. That's another twelve days sailing from London, unless you want to use the Power travel spell." He grimaced at the thought of using it.

Power travel was a spell that Captain Nolan had recently found in an antique seaman's journal. It caused a ship to travel a distance in half the time it normally would. Much to his chagrin, only Nolan had been able to cast it. Before finding it he'd been able to ignore his gifts most of the time. The spell changed all that. It used him as the locus as it enveloped the ship in a veil of power. It felt as if a fire churned inside of him and it left him debilitated for quite some time after he dropped it. He hated it, but it was a useful tool in emergencies.

The one main drawback was that it cut off all forms of electronic communication including radio, radar and cell phones. Pierce had to take command of the ship and make certain that the crew was on top of things when the spell was dropped in case of other ships were in the area. That was the primary reason that he insisted that it only be used in deep water. Near coastlines they were more at risk of a collision. Why this didn't happen during the spell was something no one understood.

"No, we won't use a big team," Sofie said. "I think Miguel and Rollie will be our Knights. We'll up the protection charms on their rings. Stealth and speed are what will be required. But, we will need to use the Power travel spell, Captain so Gordon, you'll need to sit this one out."

Sofie looked at Pierce who nodded in understanding. "There won't be any snakes to charm," he said, a smile touching his lips.

"Time isn't on our side," Caroline said. "By the time we reach London, we'll only have another week for the team to contact Anna and persuade her to come with them."

"But we don't need to wait," Anya said. "I have more than enough to pay for our airfares and hotels. We can contact Anna as soon as we find her."

It grew quiet for a moment. The captain, Rollie and Miguel looked at Anya, then at the Ladies.

"Anya," Agnes said. "You can't go with the team. I know you feel you need to be directly involved, but,"

"But, I'm too old. Is what you mean?" Anya asked.

"Yes," Sofie said. "It's cruel to say so, but remember that Anna's life is at stake. We must move quickly. And while the team gets to Anna, you will wait with us in Milan and then lead us to 'Freiheit Dorf'. I think it will be there that the greatest danger will appear and it will be up to you to guide Anna if she's to open the portal into Sanctuary."

Anya was quiet for a long time. Finally, she looked at Rollie and Miguel.

"You find Anna for me," She said. "Promise that you'll keep her safe and bring her to me."

"We will," Rollie said. "Count on it."

Chapter Eleven: The Dark One Waits

"I am most displeased," Gustav said. "How did your Dark Hunters come to lose an old woman after you vaunted their prowess over Karl's efforts?" He eyed the figure lurking in the darkened corner of the office with the contempt he felt.

"Do not criticize what you do not understand, old man," The Baron said. "My Hunters almost ran her to ground. It was entirely due to the interference of some powerful mages that she escaped. Those that let the Light Ones prevail are no longer. Those that remain will not make the same mistake."

"So, where is she now?" Gustav asked.

"It is more important to find where the amulet has been kept for so many years and who is supposed to claim it now," the Baron said. "I have long sought it, far longer than you. That woman hid it well. But, the time is near for it to reappear. I feel it. And, when it does, I will know it and know where it is. Then.."

"Then, what?" Gustav interrupted. "You plan to take it for your own purpose."

"For both of our purposes," the Baron said. "We will use the Wielder to open the portal into Sanctuary. You will become young and be able to walk again. You will become the leader of a force that will rule the world."

"Many have attempted to do that," Gustav said. "Alexander the Great, Napoleon, Hitler. While they had initial success, in the end, they all failed."

"None of those you mention had the power of Remka's Light aiding them," the Baron said. "With the amulet in our hands, we cannot fail."

Gustav looked at the greed showing on the Baron's face and was repulsed. He'd need to have Karl step up his efforts to find the woman before the Baron and his Dark Hunters could. As if his thoughts had been a call, Karl entered the room.

"Mien Herr," he started then realized that Gustav wasn't alone. "Who are you? How did you get in here?"

"Never mind who he is, Karl," Gustav said. "He's here at my invitation to help in the search for Anya Steadman. Do you have any news?"

Karl hesitated. He had some information, but it was for Gustav's hearing only.

"The woman was traced going from Boston to New York via a sea plane. Two men accompanied her. They took a taxi to a pier, but our investigator lost her. There was a disturbance. Some riot or fight that ended with an explosion. Our investigator had to leave the area or be detained by the police as a possible witness. By the time the police had left, the woman had disappeared."

"Pity," Gustav said. "I trust that the search will continue?"

"Of course, mien Herr," Karl said.

"Is there anything else?" Gustav asked.

"Nothing about the search," Karl said. It was a lie, but a necessary one given the stranger in the room. "There are some business concerns that need your review before implementation," he said. That was a code he hoped the old man would remember.

"Very well," Gustav said. "If you will excuse us for a few minutes Baron." Gustav looked at the Baron who inclined his head acknowledging the request.

"I will return when there is news," the Baron said. He strode across the richly carpeted room keeping out of the direct sunlight shinning through the windows. The glance he gave Karl left no doubt that he knew Karl had lied and that the lie would not be forgotten. He closed the office door so softly that it was almost a promise of things to come.

Gustav sighed wishing he'd never gotten involved with the Baron. He knew that in the end, he would be betrayed.

"Very well, Karl," he said. "What else have you?"

"The riot I mentioned," Karl said. "Besides the explosion, there was an injured man. Per our investigator, the injured man was one of the men accompanying the Steadman woman and it was he who was responsible for the blast. The investigator doesn't know how it was accomplished. He said that he saw the man approach four dark shapes in the fog. They were attempting to encircle the woman. They were chanting something he couldn't understand. The injured man raised his arms over his head and said a single word. Then the air lit up with green fire. Our investigator was pushed or thrown off his feet. By the time he was able to stand up and clear his vision, the fight was over. The four shapes were gone and the man was unconscious on the ground".

"And what happened to this man?" Gustav asked, not really caring.

"He is currently under medical care in our safe room," Karl said.

Gustav looked at Karl in disbelief. "He's here?" he asked.

"Yes," Karl said. "The investigator and his men got the man away from the dock before the police reached the scene. He called me and I had a private jet fly them to Munich and a car bring them here. Dr. Mertz has been treating him, but as of fifteen minutes ago, he was still unconscious."

"So, we have a possible means to acquire the whereabouts of the Steadman woman," Gustav said.

"You mean a hostage?" Karl asked.

"Hostage or informant," Gustav said. "Let me know immediately when he regains consciousness. I want to question him myself."

"Gustav," Karl said. "That would be most taxing. Why not let me question him? I can bring you the information?"

"No, Karl," Gustav said. "Time is running out and I must see his face, his eyes, to know that he tells the truth. If he was with her, he will know where she is or where she was going. I need to find her first. She must tell me where the amulet is. I must get to it before the Baron or he will take it for himself and I will never get to Sanctuary."

Hearing Gustav's words greatly saddened Karl. He knew that Gustav had become dangerously unstable, yet he couldn't do anything to stop this madness. He was involved too deeply to abandon the old man now. He also feared this Baron who appeared to have a hold on the old man. "I will bring you word immediately when our prisoner is awake," Karl said. He turned and left the office before Gustav said anything.

He walked across the reception room to a private elevator feeling more uneasy with each step. He looked over his shoulder half expecting to see someone following him. No one was there. The private elevator doors opened and he stepped in. Pulling a keycard he kept on a chain around his neck, he swiped it against a lock scanner then pressed a blank button on the floor selection pad. The doors closed and he was whisked down to the lowest sub-level of the building. Four stories below ground, steel reinforced concrete, it was the most secure, non-military location in the country. Very, very few individuals had access to this level. Only Gustav, Karl and Dr. Mertz had access to the room where the prisoner was held. It was to that room Karl was headed. Yet he paused. A sound like a soft breath made him turn and look back the way he'd come. His imagination almost painted a faint mist hovering near the elevator door. He blinked and it was gone. He shook his head and turned back to the door at the end of the corridor.

Karl again swiped his keycard and the steel door opened. Inside was a fully furnished apartment with a living room, kitchen and dining area, an office, bedrooms and a small medical facility. It was to this facility that he was headed. He opened the door and found the white-coated doctor bending over a form lying on a hospital bed.

Hearing someone entering the room, the doctor looked up. Short, balding with a middle-aged paunch, he didn't appear to be one of the world's foremost specialists in geriatric medicine. Yet, that was exactly what Dr. Mertz was and until today, his sole patient had been Herr Gustav Vogel.

"What have you to report?" Karl asked.

"I don't have anything to report," the doctor said. "I don't know what's wrong with this man. He's in very excellent physical condition. There is no evidence of trauma or head injury. There is no indication of infection. No fever. Yet, he is unconscious and I don't know why."

The doctor looked down at the dark face resting on the pillow. "You said that he was found at a pier," he said. "He could be off from some ship that had been in an exotic port. This leaves either some new contagion or some drug he consumed. I have drawn more blood and will have it tested with these options in mind."

"Very well," Karl said. "Please do so with all haste. Herr Vogel is getting impatient."

"That's not good," the doctor said. "I will go and check on him while the tests are running."

"What of this man?" Karl asked. "What if he wakes while you are gone?"

"I have him restrained to the bed," the doctor said. "Even if I were here, he could awaken and be disoriented. I did not want him to be injured or to have him injure me. I will return as quickly as possible." He picked up the blood vials that were on the bedside tray and left.

Karl stared at the man, willing him to wake up. "Who are you?" he asked. "What do you know?"

"Exactly my questions," the Baron said, suddenly appearing at the foot of the bed.

"How did you get in here?" Karl asked, startled.

"With you," the Baron said. "You see I never really left the office. You told Gustav that you had information about the woman and that you had acquired a prisoner. I wished to see him for myself so I followed you here, even though you didn't see me." He smiled and Karl felt chilled.

"It appears that this man is under a spell of trance," the Baron said. "Not one that my Dark Hunters placed on him. No, this is one I have never encountered and I find it very interesting. Like Gustav, I should very much like to question him. I doubt that the good doctor will be able to do anything to bring him back to consciousness, but time will tell."

Turning, the Baron's eyes caught and looked deeply into Karl's. "You will tell me immediately when this man awakens, even before you advise Herr Vogel. I will question him and get any information he has about the Steadman woman and the amulet and be long gone before Vogel knows."

"I will tell you immediately," Karl said, unable to look away.

"Good," the Baron said. "Now, escort me to the elevator and then return to watch over our prisoner. I will wait in Vogel's flat. Come to me there."

"Yes, mien Herr," Karl said. He opened the door and held it for the Baron to precede him and as told, escorted him to the elevator.

Chapter Twelve: Escape from Darkness

The scented smoke drifted up to the woven reed ceiling of the darkened hut. Soft drumbeats accompanied the chants of the mystic standing in front of the fire. Another handful of powder from the bag hanging from a belt around his middle was cast into the flames causing them to flare. The young boy sitting next to the fire flinched but then watched the smoke, seeking the images that would foretell his future. His awareness of the present world dimmed as he looked deeper and saw the blackness of evil to come.

The examination room was silent except for the whisper of the air flowing out of the overhead vent. Into this silence Umar's essence probed. The trance he'd put himself into after dealing with the four Dark Hunters lifted as he realized that he was not at his master's side but was truly alone and far away. He opened his eyes, blinking in the glare of the bright, overhead lights. Without moving, he looked around the room, memorizing everything he saw. He attempted to move his arms and found them immobilized by restraints, his legs, as well. Nothing he couldn't get out of, given enough time, but how much time did he have? None at all was the answer.

The door opened and a man entered. Umar did not pretend to still be unconscious. Instead, he looked closely at the man. Almost like a veil draped over the man, Umar could sense a dark, encompassing spell of compulsion. He could also tell that the man was struggling underneath the spell, trying to throw it off.

"You're awake," the man said tonelessly. "I must tell the Baron immediately." He turned to leave. Umar realized that he'd have only one chance.

"Wait," Umar said, using all the voice control he had. "Look at me." The man paused and looked back at Umar.

"I must tell the Baron," the man began.

"Look closely at me," Umar said. "You must not tell the Baron. He is evil. You know this. You are not evil."

While speaking, he was trying to get the man to look into his eyes. If he could do that then he could place a counter spell on the man, leaving him free to make his own choices.

"He is evil," the man said. Umar could feel the struggle going on within the man.

"Look at me," Umar said, again but softer and more urgently. The man did and Umar was finally able to lock eyes with him. "Ukombozi!" Umar commanded, his ring emitting a bright, green light directly into the man's eyes. "Release from the evil and be free."

The man staggered against the bed and grabbed the rail to keep from falling. He stood, breathing hard, eyes closed for several moments. "What happened?" he asked.

"You were be-spelled by the Baron," Umar said.

"Yes, the Baron commanded me," the man said, shaking his head to clear his thoughts. "He had no right to command me," sudden anger shown on his face as he glanced at Umar. "I am not his follower!"

"No, you are not evil," Umar said, again.

"What am I saying?" the man asked, shaking his head. "Who are you?"

"I am one who can save you," Umar said. "I can protect you from the Baron and his Dark Hunters. Who are you?"

"My name is Karl," he said, still sounding confused. "I am the assistant to Herr Gustav Vogel."

"Then Herr Vogel is in danger from the Baron, too," Umar said. "We must try to stop him from using either of you any more than he already has."

There was a long moment while Karl thought. Then, he reached over and unbuckled the restraints. "I'll call security to meet us in Herr Vogel's office. They can remove this Baron and turn him over to the police."

"I'm afraid that won't work," Umar said. "The Baron isn't really human anymore. He cannot be removed by simply having him arrested."

"What are you saying?" Karl asked. "He's an evil man but not some otherworldly creature."

"I'm afraid you're wrong," Umar said. "But we don't have time to go into it now. We must get out and find a way to get to your Herr Vogel."

Karl stopped and looked closely at Umar. He seemed to be uncertain about something but then made up his mind. He dropped his gaze and took a breath.

"I must tell you about Gustav, Herr Vogel, I mean," Karl said. "He's a very old man and I'm afraid that he's become demented. He talks about a magic amulet and a portal into a mystical land where the people will heal him so that he can walk again. He then wants to return and become like Hitler. He thinks that this magic amulet will give him the power to do all that. He's been searching for a woman he says has possessed the amulet for decades. I'm afraid what he might do if he finds her. Even more, I'm afraid what this Baron would do. I think he will take everything Gustav has and then throw him away like a used rag."

"You're absolutely correct," Umar said. "That's just what he would do. But even more, he'd use the power he took from the amulet and the resources of Herr Vogel to become a world power. He's attempted to do this many times over the centuries."

"Centuries?" Karl asked, frowning in his confusion. "How can that be?"

"Karl," Umar said. "You fear the Baron, but not enough. You must understand that there are both Light and Dark powers and the Baron is an emissary of the Dark. I saw him in a vision when I was a child. Once he was as human as you or I, but he gave himself to the Dark and became something else. He seeks out those with Power and devours their essence. He finds those who will be of use to him and deceives them into thinking he will help them to achieve their dreams. Then he abandons them when they can no longer serve his purposes. He thrives on chaos and pain. I've heard of his acts that span throughout time. Wars and all manner of evil, he stands behind them."

Umar didn't say that he was certain that Karl's Herr Vogel was already lost to the Darkness. It was Karl who was still at risk. Whatever happened, Umar would do everything he could to protect Karl, even if he never made it back to the Happenstance.

"Then let's go," Karl said. "We must save Gustav."

"We'll go, but we must use caution," Umar said. "The Baron is more powerful than you can imagine. We can't attack him directly. He'd wipe us out like swatting insects. No, we must use all of our wits and find a way to get to Herr Vogel and remove him from the Baron's influence."

The men left the medical facility and walked to the security door. Karl opened it and looked out into the hall. It appeared to be empty, but Umar also looked using not only his eyes and ears but also his arcane senses. He found the hall empty but halted Karl from exiting. He needed more information. "Tell me about the building," he said. "Where are we and where is Herr Vogel likely to be?"

"This is the safe room," Karl said. "Or rather the safe floor. We are four stories underground, surrounded by steel reinforced concrete. There is only the one elevator and only Gustav, Dr. Mertz and I have access to it. There is a staircase for emergency use but there are alarms that will trigger if any of the doors are opened. Gustav has a flat and an office on the top floor. That is where he will be."

"Is there another way into his office? Umar asked.

"There is the public access used by visitors and guests," Karl said. "They must be expected or they'll never get past all of the checkpoints. Then, there is this private elevator and a set of stairs between my office and Gustav's. His flat is beyond his office."

"How do the checkpoints work?" Umar asked.

"The first is on the street level," Karl said. "The reception desk checks a list of expected guests and who they are to see. Most don't get into Gustav's office. He has a host of directors and managers that take care of running the day-to-day business. If the guest is expected and on the list to see Gustav then the receptionist phones my assistant who will come and escort them to my office by the public elevator. For the past several years, I have taken care of these visitors myself. I can only think of two who actually got in to see Gustav."

"Who were they?" Umar asked.

"One was a professor of history and the other was a bishop," Karl said. "Wait. There was a third. It was a woman. A fortuneteller, I think. Gustav wouldn't allow me to stay in the office while he spoke with them, so I don't know what was discussed. But now, I think the woman may have put him in contact with the Baron."

"Does this elevator stop at the floor where your office is located?" Umar asked.

"Yes," Karl said. "It can stop at all of the floors in the building. Gustav used to visit the offices to show some support to his employees. He hasn't done that in quite some time."

"If you stepped off the elevator with me in tow as if I were an expected guest, how would your assistant react?"

"He might check my calendar and remind me if I have an appointment that would conflict with an unscheduled meeting, then ask if we want coffee or tea," Karl said.

"I'd prefer coffee and maybe a sandwich," Umar said, smiling. "You might say that you were not to be disturbed for the next hour. Then, we can plan."

Karl thought for a minute then grinned. "What kind of sandwich?" he asked, swiping his keycard against the elevator's lock.

Umar straightened his clothes while the elevator rose and stepped out with Karl appearing as if he belonged. As Karl had said, the assistant checked Karl's calendar and asked about coffee. Karl ordered the coffee and sandwiches and stated that he and his guest were not to be disturbed for the next hour. Once the door was closed, Karl collapsed onto his desk chair.

"Now what?" Karl asked.

"Now, we eat and plan how we can get into and out of Herr Vogel's flat," Umar said, sitting in a guest chair across from Karl. Each man was silent for several minutes, trying to think of what they could do. Karl's assistant knocked and entered with a tray of coffee and sandwiches. Umar sighed with satisfaction. He picked up a sandwich and took a bite. "So, how would you suggest we get into Herr Vogel's flat?" he asked.

"Getting in is easy," Karl said. "I generally use the staircase from my office directly into Gustav's. Getting into his private flat isn't a problem either. I have complete access."

"So, basically we can just walk right in," Umar said.

"Yes," Karl agreed. "But, it's getting out that'll be the problem. I don't think Gustav will be at all willing. Nor will the Baron, if he's still there."

"Can you call for Herr Vogel's car to be waiting?" Umar asked, looking intently into the depths of his ring, willing his power to flow into it. "Also, I assume that there is a private jet. Can you have it ready to leave at a moment's notice? I foresee that our journey leads to Milan."

"Of course," Karl said. "What are you suggesting? That we just walk in, grab Gustav and leave?"

"Basically, yes," Umar said.

"Gustav is very old," Karl said. "His heart is weak. Too much excitement may well kill him."

"We'll be as careful and move as quickly as possible," Umar said. Privately, he thought that if Herr Vogel did die, it would be a better ending than what the Baron would plan. He had Karl order the car to be waiting out in front of the office and also the jet to be ready for immediate takeoff. He then had Karl pick up his telephone receiver and speak as if he were talking with Herr Vogel while Umar opened the office door. "Yes, Herr Vogel," Karl said. "We'll be right up." Karl hung up and walked with Umar out of his office to the staircase. Neither looked at Karl's assistant.

"Mien Herr," the assistant said. "Your appointment with the head of.."

"Cancel and reschedule," Karl snapped. "Something has come up."

"Yes, mien Herr," the assistant said, obviously stung by Karl's tone.

Karl swiped his keycard in the lock at the top of the stairs and opened the door to Herr Vogel's office. No one was present so he motioned Umar to follow him. He called the private elevator and locked the door open before crossing the office and opening the door to Vogel's living quarters.

Herr Vogel was sitting in his wheelchair next to his small dining table, a blank expression on his face. The Baron was sitting behind the table with his feet up, a glass of brandy in his hand.

"Ah, Karl," the Baron said. "Has our guest finally awoken?"

"Yes," Karl said, walking to stand next to Herr Vogel. "I brought him with me."

"Excellent," the Baron said. "Bring him in."

"I am in," Umar said, stepping over the threshold. Silently, he had been preparing a shield to protect him from any initial spell that the Baron might attempt to put on him.

The Baron flicked his fingers at Umar, expecting him to fall to his knees. He frowned as he realized that his little charm didn't work. Before he could remove his feet from the tabletop, Karl grabbed Herr Vogel's wheelchair and ran with it to the open door. Umar slammed the door behind them and muttered 'Muhuri', sealing the door. He knew it would only last moments, but maybe it would give them enough time to reach the elevator. He ran after Karl and Herr Vogel onto the elevator just as the doors closed.

Herr Vogel appeared to be in a stupor. He said nothing until they reached the ground floor and went outside to the waiting limousine.

"Karl?" Herr Vogel said. "What are you doing? Where's the Baron?"

"Just hold on for another minute and I'll tell you everything, sir," Karl said, maneuvering the wheelchair so he could get Herr Vogel into the car. It was a massive vehicle equipped with a ramp to accommodate the wheelchair and clamps to hold it in place while the car was in motion. The chauffeur had been holding the car door open and assisted with the clamps. Then he looked expectantly at Herr Vogel for instructions.

"Sorry, friend," Umar said. "But, you won't be coming with us." He doubled his fist and sent the driver spinning while he got behind the wheel of the car. "Get in and hold on," he yelled at Karl.

Umar floored the gas pedal and the big vehicle took off, but not as quickly as he had wanted. From his rearview mirror he spotted the Baron run out of the building lobby and raise his hand to cast a spell. Umar made a quick left turn to get out of sight of the Baron and hoped that they could accelerate quickly enough to get out of range before being caught by the Baron.

"Take the next right and then a left," Karl yelled from the backseat. He was holding Herr Vogel's struggling arms to keep him from releasing the clamps. "Two kilometers further is the gate to the private airstrip."

Umar didn't reply, but nodded to show he'd heard. Following Karl's instructions, the car pulled through the gate and stopped next to the jet.

"Karl!" Herr Vogel cried. "What are you doing?"

"Saving your life," Karl said.

Umar opened the passenger door and Karl pushed the wheelchair out.

"Herr Vogel is very ill," Umar said to the waiting flight attendant. "He's delirious. We are taking him to a specialist. Help to get him on board."

"Do it," Karl commanded when the attendant hesitated. "Time is critical."

"Easy, mien Herr," Umar said. "We'll take care of you."

"No!" Gustav yelled. "They are kidnapping me. Stop them! You must!"

"Yes, mien Herr" Karl said. "We must get you to the hospital in Milan without delay. Dr. Mertz was away when this fit came over Herr Vogel. He said he'd call ahead so everything would be in readiness for Herr Vogel's arrival at the hospital."

The flight attendant, still confused over who was giving the orders stood still for another moment then Vogel attempted to stand up. He gasped and fell forward into Karl's arms, unconscious.

"Help me with him, you idiot," Karl said. Moving in front of the attendant, Umar gently picked the old man up and climbed up the steps into the jet. He laid the man on a bed that had been custom built at the rear of the jet and pulled a safety web across his body.

"Secure his wheelchair," Karl said to the attendant who was closing the hatch. "Let's get going and hope he makes it to Milan."

Both Karl and Umar took seats and buckled themselves in while the jet's engines began to roar and they moved to the runway. Shortly, they were airborne.

"Is there a phone on this craft?" Umar asked.

"Yes," Karl said, pointing at the wall. "Who are you calling?"

"I'm not," Umar said. "You will. You need to contact the hospital in Milan and make arrangements to take in Vogel. We'll need to use his ranting as a cover for a few days, as if he has dementia. I will contact my Ladies as soon as possible and they can make other arrangements."

"I truly think he does have dementia," Karl said. "But, won't they need a doctor's order to admit him?"

"Aren't you able to use Vogel's authority to get what's needed?" Umar asked. "I doubt that if you order a private suite with twenty-four hour medical staff that we'll be turned away."

"But what about the doctors and nurses?" Karl asked. "Medical ethics won't permit them to go along with participating in a rouse. After all, we actually did kidnap Gustav."

Don't worry," Umar said. "They'll observe what we want them to and won't be able to talk about it. Besides, we only need to hold this deception for a few days."

Chapter Thirteen: Finding Anna

Rollie and Miguel stood waiting for the shuttle bus that would take them from the Denver airport to the car rental office. It had been a long three days since they'd left the Happenstance docked in London. Both men were tired but they were still alert to their surroundings. They couldn't afford to be identified by Dark Hunters while they were looking for Anna.

"Only four days," Rollie said. "Just four more days to find Anna while we keep hidden, then convince her to believe in a magic amulet and come away with two, complete strangers."

"That's what we live for, amigo," Miguel said. "Come on. Let's get the car and go to the hotel. We'll start fresh in the morning."

Rollie was too tired to say anything, so he just nodded his head. He hoped that they could get some sleep, too. He didn't feel up to dealing with any emergencies tonight. Fortunately, they didn't need to. They picked up their car and arrived at their hotel without any problems.

"I'll put in a call to the ship to let them know we are on scene," Miguel said. He punched the numbers into his cell phone, but only heard dead air. "No go," he said. "The ship must be in Power travel mode. We're on our own."

"Won't they be coming out of it soon?" Rollie asked.

"It's such a long distance that they'll have to take it in multiple hops," Miguel replied. "The Ladies won't risk the Captain burning himself out. So, we won't know when the spell is cast and when they are clear. Best to just get on with our mission and surprise them when we get to Italy."

They were up early to begin their search. Rollie had purchased a laptop during one of their layovers, so he was able to connect to the hotel's Internet system. He tried the simplest search first and entered Anna's name, but the only result that came back was for her college's alumni association. He decided to try to search for family connections. He entered her father's name and immediately came up with a website showing 'Steadman Furniture and Appliance, George Steadman III, Proprietor'. With that was the address and telephone number.

"Got her father's business information," Rollie said.

"That easily?" Miguel asked.

"The wonder of computers," Rollie said. "Too easy?"

"Maybe," Miguel said. "If you found it so fast, the Dark Hunters could, too. They may already have him under observation."

"Can Dark Hunters use computers?" Rollie asked.

"I don't honestly know," Miguel said. "But, I think we should assume that they might be able to."

"Which means we'll need to be doubly cautious," Rollie said. "Should we invoke the misdirection incantation Miss Sofie gave us?"

"I don't want to use it unless it's life or death," Miguel said. "Using that type of spell too often gives the Dark Hunters time to find ways to counter it. It's best when used unexpectedly. I think we'll use normal surveillance for now."

Rollie nodded. Miguel was far more experienced, so it was a good idea to listen to him.

"Shall we go pay George a visit?" Rollie asked.

"I think so," Miguel replied. "I feel the need to refurnish my cabin."

"Not without asking Miss Agnes first," Rollie said. "She'd turn you into a mouse and feed you to Mr. Pierce's snake."

Both men laughed. Rollie shut down the laptop and put it into a backpack but before heading for the door, he looked out the window at the mountains just to the west of the city. "I wish I could get up and feel the power of those mountains," he said.

"I know," Miguel said. "The ship is sealed against losing our powers and all, but it isn't the same as drawing up from the earth." He stood for a moment at Rollie's side also looking at the range of mountains.

"I never knew, but it's like a hunger," Rollie said.

"Si, amigo but we can't do anything about it now," Miguel said, clapping Rollie's shoulder. "Let's go."

The men drove to Steadman's store that was actually a rather large warehouse.

"Looks like a converted aircraft hanger," Rollie said.

"Good," Miguel said. "It'll be easier to remain unnoticed with lots of furniture to duck behind."

"Wait!" Rollie said. "Over by that loading dock. A shadow within the shadow."

"Good catch," Miguel said. "Looks like we won't be shopping for furniture today. They've got the father under surveillance."

"Which means that they may already have found Anna," Rollie said.

"I don't think so," Miguel said. "If they'd found her, they wouldn't need a watch on the father. He's not the one they're after. They may just be watching anyone with the family name of Steadman and not really know if they have the right person."

"So, what should we do now?" Rollie asked.

"I think we need to see what the computer can come with on Anna herself," Miguel said. "There must be more than just the one entry."

"Won't the Dark Hunters have already done that?" Rollie asked.

"Probably," Miguel said. "But, Dark Hunters aren't the most subtle beings. They'd most likely grab on the first piece of information and run with it. We may catch something they missed."

"Alright," Rollie said. "Let's find a coffee shop where we can connect to the internet."

After finding a shop the men spent some time hours attempting to research Anna's life.

"She's practically a non-entity," Rollie said. "She has no social media presence. Her college shows that she graduated with an associates degree in accounting and that's it."

"Huh," Miguel grunted. "I honestly can't see a Wielder keeping the books for a company. She should have had been drawn toward something that would compliment her powers. Wonder why she chose such a path?"

Rollie's eyes opened wide as he realized something.

"Company," He said. He typed on the keyboard then clicked on a link. "Got her!" he said.

"How?" Miguel asked, leaning over Rollie's shoulder.

"The thing about computer searches is that you get a bunch of incorrect results. It's how the computer prioritizes the search results. George Steadman's store came up due to the Steadman name association. But, so did a bunch of companies that supply his store. There is one that manufactures outdoor furniture and for some reason, there's a link for it on the Steadman store's website. That manufacturer's website lists the owner and the employees. Anna is shown as an office assistant."

"Are you certain it's our Anna?" Miguel asked.

"Well, we can't be absolutely sure until we make contact," Rollie said. "But, the name's right and there's the furniture connection. It's a bit slim, but.."

"But, it's a lead," Miguel said. "Let's check it out. And Rollie, don't discount your instincts. They're what makes you the extraction expert."

"Some expert," Rollie said. "If I hadn't been so anxious to find her, I'd have been more thorough earlier."

"But, there was some good," Miguel said. "We know for certain that the Dark Hunters are here. That's an advantage."

They drove to the address listed on the website. The building was located in an industrial park north of the downtown area. Miguel found a place to park where they could observe the business door and the driveway.

"I'm not sensing any Dark Hunters nearby," Rollie said, looking at his ring. He saw only the normal green flicker deep in the middle.

"Neither am I," Miguel said.

"Okay," Rollie said. "Should we go inside?"

"No," Miguel said. "We wait. It's getting close to noon. People will start going to lunch soon. Hopefully, we'll be able to spot her leaving and follow her."

The afternoon sun was hot, so Miguel had rolled down the car windows. The door of the business opened and three people stepped out. Two young, fair-haired women and a man with sweat already beaded on this baldhead.

"You little dunce," the man yelled. "Why didn't you tell me Carter had called? I've been waiting all morning to talk with that guy."

"I tried to page you in the back warehouse, Mr. Pace," the woman nearest to the man said. "You didn't answer and Mr. Carter said he couldn't wait. I left a message on your desk and told you first thing when you got back to the front office."

"That's the truth," the other woman said.

"You keep out of this," Pace said. He turned back to the woman he'd been yelling at. "You screw up one more time and you're out of here. I don't care if your old man is a big customer. I only took you on to help him out, anyway."

Pace turned and locked the office door leaving the two women standing and stomped off across the parking lot. He got into a large, red car and took off. The woman Pace had yelled at began to cry and the other wrapped an arm around her shoulders trying to offer some comfort.

Rollie felt certain that the crying woman was Anna and he felt a surge of anger at Pace's treatment of her. He already thought of her as his rescue, that it was his duty to protect her.

"That's our girl," Miguel said, confirming Rollie's gut feeling. "Administrative assistants answer phones. A father who owns a furniture store and deals with manufacturers might ask the favor of employing their daughter in exchange for a large purchase or better contract. Who knows? But, that's Anna."

"I agree," Rollie said. "Looks like they were getting ready to leave. Must only work half days on Wednesdays. So, do we follow her?" He had to tamp down an urge to make contact right now.

"Yes," Miguel said. "Once we know her living and commuting arrangements we can set up a monitoring schedule."

The men waited and listened while the other woman got Anna calmed.

"I swear," the woman said. "That man is such a jerk!"

"Why is he like that?" Anna asked, wiping her tears on the backs of her hands.

"Because he's a jerk, born and bred," the woman said. "But, this is the end. I'm going to quit before he starts in on me again. I might clout him."

"But Irene," Anna said. "What'll I do if you leave?

"Leave too," Irene said. "Find another job. You've got what it takes to really get ahead, but not here. Pace and quite frankly, your father, are holding you back. Chuck it! Figure out what you'd like to do with your life and go after it."

Rollie smiled at Irene's words. She had no idea how Anna's life would change in the coming days. But, her words, meant to be positive, had the opposite effect on Anna. She appeared to be terrified.

"Hey!" Irene said, giving Anna's shoulders a bit of a shake. "Buck up. Let's get out of here and go get a drink. We'll talk about the next phases of our lives."

"I..I can't," Anna stuttered. "I promised my mother that I'd babysit for her neighbors. I can't disappoint her."

"Anna," Irene said, shaking Anna's shoulders again. "In case on one's told you, you're a grown woman. You have your own apartment, you pay your own bills and you have the right to live your own life. Call the neighbors and tell them something's come up so you need to cancel. I promise you that the world won't end."

Anna didn't reply immediately, but then she seemed to make a decision.

"Alright," Anna said. "I do need to go home first. But, I'll meet you."

"Nope," Irene said. "You'll get home then back out of coming. We go now. How about Peter's Place? Come on, or we'll miss the bus."

"Rats!" Miguel said. "They ride a bus. That's going to make it harder to follow Anna."

"I could get on the bus and ride with them," Rollie said.

"Can you check your cell phone and see if there's a bar called Peter's Place?" Miguel asked.

Rollie made the search and found that there was such a place. It was across town.

"Do we assume that this is the Peter's Place Irene wants to go to?" Rollie asked.

"I think so," Miguel said. "It would be best to get there ahead of them."

"Okay," Rollie said. "Let's go."

He read off the address and Miguel started the car.

"You know," Rollie said. "Now that we've found her, I don't like letting her out of our sight."

"You bond with people so easily," Miguel said. "It's part of your gift."

"Mmm," Rollie muttered. He'd never felt that he had much of a gift. He just listened to people and only said what they really needed to hear. It was much like what his mother did with her patients.

"Do we make contact with Anna today?" he asked.

"I don't think so," Miguel said. "If you recall, Anya said that she believed that the law firm would trace Anna. They'd most likely use a private investigator to do this."

"That's probably correct," Rollie said. "Many law firms have investigators on retainers so they can call them as needed."

"What would happen if the investigator was called out of town?" Miguel asked.

"They'd need to get someone else," Rollie said, wondering where this was heading.

"Right," Miguel said. "That someone being you. Your father's a detective, right? Could you pass yourself off as a P.I.?

"I'd thought about becoming an investigator before the Ladies contacted me," Rollie said. "I'd need to brush up on the latest requirements and get a license. Any law firm would want to vet me."

"Rollie," Miguel said. 'You're thinking like a regular person. Think like a Knight."

Rollie blushed then laughed.

"I guess I was," he said.

"If you're to become the investigator, Anna can't see you now," Miguel said.

"Yeah," Rollie said. "Let me out where I can get a taxi. I'll go back to the hotel and see what I can find out about the law firm."

"Right," Miguel said. "I'll follow her to her home and see what we're up against there."

"I hope Irene can convince her to quit working for that slob," Rollie said. "No one should have to take that kind of abuse."

Chapter Fourteen: Rolland Jones, P.I.

Rollie had studied the web site for the law firm of Higley and Carter. There were photographs of the senior partners as well as the junior associates. But, there were none for the office staff. This meant that Rollie would need to watch who went to the office daily in order to determine who worked there and who might be their investigator. That would take too long. He called Miguel.

"Miguel," Rollie said. "I've got to get into that office if I'm going to find out who they use as an investigator."

"Yes," Miguel said. "I can feel that we're running out of time. I think we'd better go ahead and break in tonight."

But, Rollie had another idea. Like Miguel, he felt that time wasn't on their side. He didn't want to wait until tonight. Instead, took a taxi to the building where Higley and Carter had their offices. He got out in front and studied the building, walked around it and made sure he knew where every door was located. Finally, he went in through the main entrance. It was late afternoon and many businesses were already closed. He needed to get into the office now. It was time to cast Miss Sofie's spell.

Rollie found an alcove at the back of the hallway outside of the law office that would hide is actions. He took a deep breath. He wasn't well versed in spell casting. It wasn't a big part of his duties and he always had to beat down his own self-doubt that he could do it. Belief was a crucial part of a successful casting. "Relax," he said. "You can do this."

He took another deep breath and slowly let it out. He looked deeply into his ring and felt power flow into it. Raising his right hand with his ring above his head, he began to softly chant. "By the Fire, by the Water, by the Earth and Air. Let all eyes notice naught, no harm to any. So, by the Rod do I invoke," He felt a tingle in his hand and then he was bathed in a momentary wash of green light. Now to see if it worked.

The office door opened and a woman stepped out. Rollie slipped around her and into the office without her noticing him. The spell worked. Rollie felt a surge of accomplishment. He could search the offices and hopefully, locate the information identifying the P.I. agency. But, he'd need to be careful moving around. If anyone heard him he'd be noticed.

Rollie started with the already deserted reception desk. He hoped that there might be files or letters that could help to identify the name of the investigator, but there were no files. There were some letters in the outgoing mail basket and he quickly sifted through them but found nothing.

He stepped into a richly paneled and carpeted hallway leading to the individual offices. He saw a door at the far end and guessed it was probably one of the senior partner's offices. "Might as well start at the top," he said to himself.

He quickly walked down the hall and stopped at the door. Gold lettering announced that the office belonged to T. Higley. Holding his breath, he listened for any sound from inside the office. Not hearing anything, he slowly opened the door.

He entered into an outer office furnished with a desk where Mr. Higley's assistant must sit. A sofa and four chairs were place near the window. Scatterings of magazines were on the end tables ready for clients' perusal. Thick carpeting muffled his footsteps as he walked to the desk. There was nothing left out on top. He tried to open the center desk drawer, but found it locked. Well, locks were something he could deal with. His father had taught him all about picking locks when he was just a boy. He pulled a zippered case from his jacket pocket and opened it. He removed a lock pick and inserted it into the lock. Within a few seconds, he had the drawer open. Only blank notepads and a selection of pens were inside.

He next opened the right hand drawer that was larger. Inside were several folders labeled with client names. He flipped through them and stopped at the fourth one. It was labeled 'Anna L. Steadman'. "Bingo!" he said, pulling out the folder and reading the contents. Everything Anya had said was there. She had left a box, contents unknown and a letter addressed to Anna with Mr. Higley to be tuned over to Anna on her twenty-fifth birthday. There was also information about the trust fund Anya had set up. Anna was going to be a very wealthy woman. Another document listed Anna's current address, as well as her work address and telephone number. There was a letterhead at the top of the report showing 'Matthew Lennox, Private Investigations'. Exactly the information Rollie had hoped to find. Lastly, there was a letter from Mr. Higley requesting Anna to come to the office to discuss the inheritance left by Anya.

Rollie closed the file and replace it in the drawer. He relocked the desk and left the office. He was about to return to the reception desk when a distinguished looking man in an expensive grey suit stepped through a door marked 'Conference Room'. Another man and a woman holding an electronic tablet followed him.

"We'll work on getting that injunction," the distinguished man said.

"Thank you, Mr. Higley," the other man said, shaking hands.

"Helen will show you out," Mr. Higley said.

Rollie froze as Mr. Higley walked toward him. The spell was still working as he was passed by without even a glance. Next was to get out of the office. He hurried after the client so he could slip out the door behind him. Retreating to the far end of the hallway, Rollie reversed the spell. He again raised his hand over his head and softly chanted. "By the Fire, by the Water, by the Earth and Air. Let all eyes see what is true, no harm to any. So, by the Rod do I invoke." Again, his hand tingled and he was bathed in green light. He walked to the elevator and pushed the down button. When the door opened and Rollie stepped on, a young woman smiled at him. Clearly, the spell was gone.

Rollie now had the address for the private investigator that the law office used. He pulled out his cell phone and began to call Miguel, then stopped. He knew what he needed to do. He must get the investigator to leave town on some pretext so that Rollie could substitute for him. How he was to accomplish it was the problem.

People were Rollie's area of expertise. He could gain trust and talk people into doing what he wanted them to do pretty easily. But, getting a trained investigator to leave Rollie in charge of his client while he was sent out of town, all without being aware he was doing it would take more than mere talk. Not hypnosis. Rollie knew how to use hypnosis but it wouldn't work. You couldn't hypnotize someone into doing something they normally wouldn't do. No, he'd need to use a spell of Compulsion.

Rollie felt his stomach muscles tighten with fear and pulled his phone out of his pocket. He understood how it was supposed to work, but he'd never cast a Compulsion spell before. He'd be in a real jam if he couldn't cast it. He knew Miguel would come and help him if he called, but that wouldn't be right. That would leave Anna without protection. Besides, if the spell was to work right, it needed to be cast one to one. He put his phone back into his pocket.

The Lennox office wasn't far from the law office so Rollie walked over, rehearsing what he'd say. He opened the office door and walked in. A pretty young woman was sitting at the reception desk. She appeared to be somewhere between eighteen and twenty years old. She looked up from the magazine she was reading and smiled.

"Hello," Rollie said, smiling in return. "Is Matt in? I was supposed to meet him at one o'clock, but I'm running late."

"Oh!" the girl exclaimed. She looked down at an old-fashioned appointment book. "I don't see an appointment listed Mr..,"

"Jones," Rollie said. "Rolland Jones Investigations. I just flew in from Boston to consult with Matt on a case. Are you sure there isn't an appointment listed? I made it a couple of days ago."

"Ah, geez!" the girl said. "He's gonna fire me. I'm sorry, but I don't remember you calling."

"Well," Rollie said. "Maybe I can smooth it over. Will you let him know I'm here, please?"

"Uh, sure," she said, grabbing the phone on the desk and pushing a button. "Mr. Lennox, Mr. Jones of Rolland Jones Investigations is here for your meeting. No sir. I made a mistake. He called earlier this week. Yes, sir."

She jumped up and hurried to open the door to the inner office. She looked upset.

"Don't worry," Rollie whispered, winking his eye at her as he entered. She nodded and closed the door.

"Mr. Lennox?" Rollie asked, extending his hand to Lennox. "I'm Rolland Jones out of Boston. Sorry about the confusion."

"No, I'm sorry," Lennox said, taking Rollie's hand. "My regular assistant is out on maternity leave and Jill is the third temp I've had in the past month."

Rollie had been studying Lennox. He was tall with an athletic build. He was around forty years old with light brown hair and eyes. He had a firm handshake and was studying Rollie in return. He indicated a chair for Rollie to sit in and returned to his desk.

"So, how may I help you?" Lennox asked.

"Well, I'm attempting to trace a relative of a client and in the course of my investigation, I found that the family may have had business with you."

Rollie had been twisting his ring to catch the light and reflect it into Lennox's eyes.

"Oh?' Lennox said. "And what's the name of the family?"

"It's Johnson," Rollie said. He noticed that Lennox's eyes were beginning to glaze.

"That's a pretty common name," Lennox said.

"Yes," Rollie said. "But, that doesn't matter. You're going to go and find someone in Hawaii named Tex."

"I will?" Lennox asked.

"Yes," Rollie said. "It's an emergency and it will take you two weeks to find him."

"I can't close the office for two weeks," Lennox said.

"You'll leave me in charge," Rollie said.

"I don't know you," Lennox said.

"You've known me for several years," Rollie said. "You'd trust me with your life and you wouldn't let anyone else take over for you."

"That's right," Lennox said. "I wouldn't trust anyone else."

"Tomorrow, you'll introduce me to Mr. Higley," Rollie said.

"Yes," Lennox said. "Tomorrow I'll introduce you."

"Good," Rollie said. "And remember, it's urgent that you find Tex in Hawaii."

"Yes," Lennox said. "It's urgent."

Rollie lowered his hand so that the light stopped reflecting from his ring. Lennox shook his head and rubbed his hand over his eyes.

"Why yes," Rollie said. "Of course I'll substitute for you. It sounds like it's an urgent case."

"It is," Lennox said. "I can't tell you how much I appreciate your help."

"Not at all," Rollie said. He stood up and waited for Lennox to join him. Lennox opened the door and stepped out ahead of Rollie.

"Jill," Lennox said. "I want you to clear my calendar. I've had an urgent matter come up and will be unavailable for the next two weeks. Mr. Jones will be handling the Higley-Carter business while I'm gone."

"Yes, sir," Jill said. "I'll let the temp agency know you won't need anyone while you're gone."

"Don't do that," Rollie said. "Someone needs to answer the phone and pass along messages."

"Yes," Lennox said. "I'll need you to stay while I'm gone."

"Sure," Jill said. She looked at Rollie and smiled her gratitude.

"So, I'll meet you at the law office tomorrow?" Rollie asked.

"Yes," Lennox said. "I have a standing appointment at eight o'clock every day with Mr. Higley to receive any assignments."

"Sounds good," Rollie said. "See you there."

Rollie left the office and called Miguel. "I'm in," he said. "Anything new?"

"No," Miguel said. "She's still at Peter's Place. I agree with you. From the way Irene has talked about their workplace, I can't wait for her to get her inheritance so she can tell that monster of a boss where he can go. Irene says that she's going to quit tomorrow morning. It sounds as if Anna is expecting him to blame her for it."

"Jerk," Rollie said. "I'll meet you at Anna's place later and bring you up to date."

"You sound exhausted," Miguel said.

"Had to do both Miss Sofie's spell and a silent spell of Compulsion," Rollie said.

"Go get some food and rest until you feel up to snuff," Rollie said. "We'll talk later."

Rollie didn't have much choice. It was one thing to perform a verbal incantation with hand and arm motions to manipulate the power flows. It was something else to perform a silent incantation. It required split concentration to maintain a verbal conversation while silently casting the spell and using only emotion to maintain it. It was intensely draining and as always, Rollie had to fight his own self-doubts. Right now, he was really beginning to feel it.

He took a taxi back to the hotel and ordered room service. He was ravenous so he didn't stint on the calories. He ordered a steak with fries along with a chocolate milkshake for medicinal purposes, or so he told himself. He sat the empty tray outside the door and went to take a nap. He was asleep within moments.

He was running, pulling Anna behind him. The full moon was rising over jagged peaks. Ahead of them was a boulder strewn valley. Behind them, Dark Hunters followed. They had to reach the base of the mountain and open the portal or they would fall to the Baron.

Rollie awoke with a start. Miguel's hand was on his arm.

"Bad dream?" Miguel asked.

"Bad sending," Rollie said. "I think I just received a nudge to move faster."

"Well, Anna's tucked in for the night," Miguel said. "So, tell me what happened to make you use a compulsion spell."

"I went to the law firm's office and used the misdirection spell to search the office. I found a file with Anna's name on it. The information in it matched what Anya said. There was a letter to be sent to Anna asking her to come to the office on her birthday to receive an inheritance. Her contact information was listed on a report from the private investigator. His name and address were listed at the top of the page, 'Matthew Lennox Investigations'. I went to the office and cast the compulsion spell on him. I substitute for him for the next two weeks for the law firm's needs. I'm to meet Lennox tomorrow morning to be introduced to Mr. Higley."

"You've made good progress," Miguel said, surprising Rollie who expected to have to justify his actions. "Rolland Jones, P.I.," Miguel said, chuckling.

Rollie smiled, but it faded as he remembered his dream. "We'll need to gain Anna's trust really fast," he said.

"You will," Miguel said. "It's what you do. You'll take care of Anna and I'll take care of you. Together, we'll get her to Anya and the Ladies. And speaking of the Ladies, I'll see if I can get a call through to them and let them know what we've found and done. I think they'll be pleased."

To say that Mr. Higley wasn't pleased with Lennox's announcement that he was going to be away and that Rollie was going to be his substitute would be quite the understatement. Higley's red face almost matched the red leather of the chair he sat in. The massive and ornate desk was large enough to lay on which would come in handy if he had an apoplectic attack and needed CPR.

"Matt!" Higley said. "You know we have that multi-million dollar inheritance case coming up in just a few days. You know the details. I need you on this."

"Mr. Higley," Lennox said. "I've known Rolland Jones for a long time. He's the only one I'd trust to take over for me."

"No offense, Mr. Jones," Higley said. "But, it's just so sudden and at a really inconvenient time."

"I understand that you're uncomfortable," Lennox said. "But, you know I wouldn't dream of going if it wasn't an urgent matter. That's why I asked my friend Jones to help out."

"Well," Higley said. "You've got to do what you must, I suppose."

"I promise that I won't let you down, Mr. Higley, Rollie said. "Could you please bring me up to speed on your current requirements?"

Higley nodded and reached for the intercom. "Helen, please bring in the Steadman file", he said.

"Yes, sir," Helen said. A few seconds later, she brought in the requested file and handed it to Higley.

"Matt can brief you on our regular cases where you might be needed, but this one is currently of prime importance," he said. He handed the file to Rollie who opened it and reread the contents as if he'd never seen them before.

"So," Rollie said. "An inheritance case. But, where do I come in? You obviously don't need anyone to trace her whereabouts."

"I've received some phone calls discretely asking if we had a Ms. Steadman as a client and I find that disturbing," Higley said. "Of course, I did not provide any information but with the amount in the trust fund, and I assure you that it is substantial, the possibility of abduction is very real. She'll need protection."

Rollie nodded. Inside, he was pleased. The situation was exactly what he needed to get close to Anna.

"I was going to mail that letter to Ms. Steadman," Higley said. "But, I think it would be better if it was hand delivered. So, I'll want you to take it to her ttomorrow and arrange to bring her here the next day."

"That sounds like a wise plan," Rollie said.

"Good," Higley said. "Matt, I wish you luck with your case and be careful. We'll see you tomorrow to pick up the letter, Mr. Jones. I don't think we'll need to meet again unless something urgent comes up."

It was clearly a dismissal, so both men left the office. Rollie stopped Lennox when they reached the sidewalk. "Good luck finding your missing man," he said, shaking hands so that he could confirm that the compulsion spell was still strongly in force. "See you in two weeks."

"Yes," Lennox said. "In two weeks."

Rollie nodded and walked down the street to find a taxi.

Chapter Fifteen: The Attack Begins

"Jones," Mr. Higley's voice growled over the phone early the next day. "We need you immediately. We've had a break-in."

"I'll be right over," Rollie said. He'd been sitting in the car outside of Anna's apartment building.

"Looks like the Dark Hunters are on the move," he said.

"It's only two days until Anna's birthday," Miguel said. "I've been expecting them to make some move. You'd better take the car and find out what the situation is at the law office. I'll ride the bus with Anna."

Miguel got out of the car and Rollie slid over to the driver's seat. It took him ten minutes to reach the office. There were police cars with flashing lights at the curb, so Rollie had to park in the next block. He had to talk his way past a police officer to get to Mr. Higley. There was evidence of vandalism all along the hallway. Doors broken open, files tossed around, equipment smashed but Rollie knew that it was all window dressing. He needed to get to Higley's office to confirm if they'd found Anna's file.

"Nothing appears to have been taken," Higley said to a police detective who was standing next to him. "Just a lot of vandalism."

"What about your security system?" the detective asked. "You have alarms and cameras."

"The security system was somehow bypassed," Higley said. "No alarms or video data."

"That means that they're tech savvy," Rollie said. "This wasn't just a smash and grab."

"And who are you?" the detective asked, eyeing Rollie with suspicion.

"This is Mr. Jones. He's an investigator the firm has on retainer," Higley said. "I called him to come. No, it wasn't a break-in to steal equipment. Our files were searched and that means some of our clients are vulnerable. But that's not the most important thing. They left Ms. Steadman's file open right in the middle of my desk. They wanted us to know that they got the information on her."

"We need to contact Ms. Steadman Immediately," Rollie said. "They have her home address."

"I know," Higley said. "The trust fund can't be released until tomorrow, but we can offer to put her up in a hotel until things get sorted out."

"Who is this Ms. Steadman?" the detective asked.

"I'll explain in a moment," Higley said. "Jones, I want you to go to her home and bring her back here today."

"Of course," Rollie said. "It would be best. But, I doubt that she'd just come with me. No proper, young woman would go off with a complete stranger."

"I'd thought of that," Higley said. "I'll have Helen go with you and bring along a letter of introduction. Hopefully, that will ease any suspicion Ms. Steadman might have."

Rollie didn't know whether to be pleased or not about having Helen tag along. He'd been planning to approach Anna by himself or with Miguel along. But, situations were fluid and keeping up with changes was necessary.

Helen came in with the letter of introduction for Higley to sign. She smiled at Rollie after Higley handed her back the letter. She folded it into an envelope with Anna's name on it and placed it into her handbag.

"Ready?" She asked Rollie.

"Yes," Rollie said. He motioned for her to precede him out the door.

Another police car was parked in front of Anna's apartment building when they arrived.

"Oh," Helen said. "We may be too late."

Rollie parked the car and they hurried into the building only to be stopped by an officer.

"We're from the offices of Higley and Carter, attorneys at law," Helen said. "I'm Mr. Higley's personal assistant and this is Mr. Jones of Lennox Investigations. We're here to see Ms. Anna Steadman."

"I'm afraid that isn't possible," the officer said.

"And why is that?" Helen asked.

"Ms. Steadman isn't here, yet," the officer said.

"Perhaps we'd better talk with the officer in charge," Rollie said.

"That would be me," an officer said from inside Anna's apartment.

Helen looked into the room and gasped. Rollie stepped up behind her and saw that the apartment had been torn apart. Cushions slashed and the stuffing pulled out. Books torn apart and pages were scattered across the floor, glassware smashed. It was a mess.

Just then Rollie heard the sound of running footsteps coming up behind him. Anna was there.

"That's my apartment," she said. "Please let me through."

Rollie and Helen stepped aside and she pushed passed the officer. Rollie studied the slender woman's reactions as she looked at the scene inside.

"Oh, no!" Anna said, covering her mouth with both hands.

"Please don't go in just yet, Ms. Steadman," the officer said. "The lab techs are still processing the scene."

"What happened?" she asked, obviously confused. "Why would someone do this? I don't have anything anyone would want."

"Anna, dear," a woman's voice called from across the hall. "I heard the ruckus and called the police. Ray let them in. The police, I mean.

That's when we found the man. He'd been beaten to within an inch of his life. They just took him to the hospital.

Rollie felt a sudden chill. They were talking about Miguel. He just knew it. But why hadn't Miguel followed Anna to work? Why hadn't he called to let Rollie know that something was happening? Didn't he trust Rollie to come to his aid? He'd failed Umar and now he'd failed another partner.

"Ms. Steadman," The officer said, jarring Rollie out of his dismal thoughts. "We need to ask you some questions. Would you please come down to the precinct with me?"

"Not without her attorney present," Helen said. "I represent Mr. Theodore Higley of Higley and Carter. I have a letter of introduction for Ms. Steadman on another issue, but unless she declines, Mr. Higley is her legal representative. I must insist on contacting him and your permitting Ms. Steadman to consult with him."

The officer looked sharply at Helen and Rollie.

"And who are you?" he asked Rollie.

"I'm Rolland Jones, representing Lennox Investigations, also representing Higley and Carter," he answered, pulling out a card case and showing the officer his 'license', actually a blank card be-spelled to show whatever he needed it to.

"A P.I.," the officer said. "Don't have much use of your type."

"You have your job, I have mine," Rollie said, his voice mild. "And right now, my job is to protect Ms. Steadman."

"Protect her from what or whom?" the officer asked.

"Let's let Mr. Higley answer that," Helen said, replacing her cell phone into her purse. "He'll meet us at the precinct. Ms. Steadman can ride with us."

The officer looked as if he was going to protest, but again, Helen cut him off.

"Is Ms. Steadman under arrest?" she asked. "She's a victim, not a suspect."

"Alright," the officer said. "I'll follow your car."

"But what about my apartment?" Anna asked. "I can't just leave it wide open."

"We'll leave an officer to guard your stuff until your super can get the door boarded up," the detective said. "Let's go."

Once in the car, Anna turned a bewildered face to Helen who sat next to her in the back seat.

"I don't understand," Anna said. "What's happening? Who are you?"

"Poor dear," Helen said. "No doubt you're confused. This wasn't supposed to happen. Mr. Jones and I were supposed to meet with you and request you to come to the offices of Higley and Carter. Mr. Higley will explain in detail, but you're the beneficiary of an inheritance, a rather substantial one. It's in the form of a trust fund set up by your great, great aunt. It's to be turned over to you on your twenty-fifth birthday."

"But what does that have to do with someone breaking into my apartment and finding an injured man inside?" Anna asked.

"I said that the inheritance was substantial," Helen said. "Unfortunately, our offices were also broken into last night. They searched our files and found out all of the particulars about you. Mr. Higley felt that you were at risk for abduction and assigned Mr. Jones to protect you. We arrived too late to prevent your place from being broken into, but fortunately, we can keep you safe."

"But why do the police want to question me at the station?" Anna asked. "That seems to indicate that they think I did something illegal."

"You haven't," Rollie said. "They're just trying to be through. But, we'll let Mr. Higley handle the cops. He'll explain everything."

They arrived at the police station and found Mr. Higley already waiting.

"Ms. Steadman," he said, shaking her hand. "I so glad to finally meet you, even under these circumstances."

"Thank you," Anna said. "But, I don't understand. They said you'd explain."

"And I will," Higley said. "But let's clear up this police business first."

They entered the station with the detective following and were directed to a small interrogation room. Anna, Higley and Helen went in, but the detective barred Rollie. He took a seat near the door to wait. He was worried about Miguel. How badly was he hurt? Why didn't his ring protect him? Should Rollie contact the Ladies?

It was almost thirty minutes later that the door opened and Anna exited, along with Higley and Helen. The officer looked concerned. "Mr. Higley," he said. "I know you think you have matters under control, but won't you reconsider having an officer guard Ms. Steadman?"

"I'm certain that Mr. Jones is more than capable of protecting her," Higley said. "Especially as no one will know where she'll be staying. I take full responsibility."

"I take it that Ms. Steadman has been cleared of any suspicion of wrong doing?" Rollie asked.

"Yes," Higley said. "Silly waste of time. As if she had time to get from her workplace to her home, wreck it, attack some stranger, then return to her work in the length of time it took for her neighbor to phone the police after hearing the disturbance." Higley shook his head in disbelief then took Anna's hand.

"I'm going to make sure that you are well protected," Higley said. "Tomorrow, we'll meet at my office and go to the bank to sign the papers turning your trust fund over to you. Also, we'll retrieve the item your great, great aunt had stored for you."

"I can't believe this is happening," Anna said. "Are you sure you have the right person? I mean I never knew I had a great, great aunt. My family never said anything about her. Maybe it's someone else you need."

"No," Higley said. "It's you. We had you investigated and we're certain that you are the Anna Lynn Steadman in question. Now, we need to get you to a safe place. Any suggestions?"

He was looking at Rollie when he asked the question. Rollie took a moment before suggesting the hotel he and Miguel were living at.

"It's where I've been staying," he said. "I think that one of the small suites would provide us with a secure place to stay for awhile."

A short time later, Anna was safely ensconced at the hotel. Helen had volunteered to bring her some clothing so she wouldn't need to return to her damaged apartment. Anna asked about calling her parents, but Rollie persuaded her that it would be a bad idea right now.

"I'd wait until after you and Mr. Higley get your business concluded," he said. "That way, you'll know what you need to deal with and will be able to make decisions accordingly."

Anna nodded and walked around the room, too nervous to sit down. Rollie wanted to calm her and started to ask her about herself. "What do you think you'd like to do when you get your trust fund?" he asked.

"I don't know," Anna said. "Probably have my parents take care of things. They're much better at that kind of thing than I am."

"Surely, there's something you've longed to do," Rollie said. "Someplace you've always wanted to go."

"Oh, I guess everyone wants to see London or Paris," she said. "But, I doubt I'll be able to go anytime soon."

She'd been pacing around the room and suddenly stopped. "Did anyone say anything about the injured man they found in my apartment?" she asked suddenly.

"No," Rollie said. "Why? Do you think you know him?"

"No," she said. "I don't know why, but I don't think he was the criminal. I'd like to help him."

Rollie hadn't expected this. He watched her face. There was sincerity. She really was concerned about Miguel.

"I'll see what I can find out about him, but he's probably under arrest," he said.

"But, I don't have to press charges, do I?" she asked.

"No, you don't," he said, almost smiling. "But, I'd wait until we know more.

"I have the feeling that there isn't much time," she said. "Can't we do something?"

"I'll tell you what," Rollie said. "When Helen gets back, she can stay with you while I go to the hospital and see what I can find out. The main thing is that we keep you out of sight for a couple of days."

"Couldn't I come with you to the hospital?" she asked.

"I don't think that would be a good idea," he said. Fortunately, Helen returned so he didn't need to continue arguing with Anna.

He was worried about Miguel's condition, too. He left Anna with Helen and drove directly to the hospital. He took the precaution of casting the misdirection spell again so he could get into Miguel's room without anyone noticing. This time, he didn't even think about failing to cast it correctly. He just did it.

The ER was extremely busy, so he needed to move with care to avoid bumping into anyone. He found the treatment room where Miguel was. As expected, there was a police officer outside the curtained room. He waited until the officer's attention was focused on an ambulance crew arriving and entered the room.

Miguel was unconscious. A bandage was wrapped around his head. He face was a mass of purple bruises and his left arm was encased in a cast. An intravenous drip was fed into his right arm and sensor wires were attached to his chest, the monitor showing his vital signs.

"Miguel?" Rollie asked softly. "Can you hear me?"

He watched for any indication that Miguel would open his eyes, but there was no reaction. Rollie took Miguel's right hand and looked at his ring. There was no flame. It was dead. What could have done that? He remembered asking a similar question and Miguel responding 'nothing good'. How right that was. Somehow the Dark Hunters found a way to drain the Knight rings of their protections.

Rollie gently released Miguel's hand and carefully left the room. He needed to find a healer and the only ones he knew were aboard the Happenstance. He knew that the Ladies would come or send Dr. Quan if he contacted them, but the knew Miguel wouldn't want that. Then, he remembered Anya's story about Remka healing the village children with her amulet. Anna would take possession of the amulet tomorrow. Maybe, just maybe, there was a way to help both Miguel and Anna.

Chapter Sixteen: Remka's Light Awakens

Rollie returned to the hotel and told Anna that he wasn't able to find out much about the injured man. He was unconscious and was being guarded by the police, most likely under arrest. But, as Rollie wasn't a relative, he wasn't given any information about his condition.

"I'm sure that when the police are able to question him, we'll find out what he was doing in your apartment," Helen said.

"I just can't help feeling that he was there to help me," Anna said. It was the sign of a Wielder of Light to be concerned about another but to sense that Miguel had been trying to help indicated a very strong power in this Wielder.

"Well, anything's possible," Rollie said. Then, for Helen he added a caution. "But, don't count on his being innocent. After all, you don't know him, so what was he doing in your apartment? It could well be a case of a falling out among thieves."

"Rollie's right, Anna," Helen said. "Mr. Higley will get the full story, then we'll know if the man is a hero or a villain."

Anna was restless the rest of the day. At her request, Rollie called the hospital to find out about Miguel's condition. He was asked if he was a relative and had to reply that he wasn't. He was told that they couldn't release any information. Rollie thanked the nurse and hung up the phone.

Rollie and Helen did their best to distract Anna. They tried to get her to talk about herself, but she was so reserved it was like pulling teeth, as Helen remarked. Rollie again asked her what she'd always wanted to do. This time, she answered.

"When I was a little girl, I thought that I wanted to be a doctor or a nurse," she said. "Maybe a veterinarian. Someone who helps people to heal."

"Did you study any medicine in school?" he asked, knowing she hadn't.

"No," she said. "My parents didn't think it was best for me. They thought that I was too, I don't know, stupid, I guess. Anyway, it was just a dream."

Rollie looked at Helen and saw the same look of anger that he was feeling. Why would anyone's parents deliberately keep their child from reaching for her dreams? Then, he remembered the conversation he'd had with his father when he told him that he was going to go to sea as a steward. The things his father had called him hadn't been far removed from being called stupid. And, while his mother didn't yell, the tears in her eyes were as hard to take as his father's cursing. Both had wanted him to follow in their footsteps. Yet, he wasn't able to tell them about how the advertisement guided him. So, he'd had to leave things hanging.

Helen struggled for a moment before she spoke. "I shouldn't tell you this," she said. "It's really not my place, but you should know that you're going to have enough money to go back to school and become a doctor or nurse. It's not too late, if it's something you'd really like to pursue. You should think about it."

Anna just shook her head. Well, maybe Remka's Light would change her mind. As a Wielder healing would be second nature. He intended her to find this out tomorrow.

Anna's birthday dawned fair and bright and the three of them made their way to Higley's office early in the morning. Rollie was careful to watch for any signs of the presence of Dark Hunters. Fortunately, they had no difficulties either at the office or going to the bank where she signed the papers that turned the trust fund over to her. She also had to meet with accountants, tax people and investment managers. Rollie expected her to be completely out of her depth, but she surprised him with her grasp of the economics. This was not a stupid or inept woman. In fact, after her initial shock of suddenly becoming rich, she began to show anticipation of what she might do.

Finally came the time Rollie had been waiting for. The bank manager had a safe deposit box brought up from the vault to his office. He took it and Anna into a conference room and left her alone. She seemed to take a long time. Rollie guessed that she was reading Anya's letter. He wondered what she thought. Then, out of the very air, a strong sensation of warmth and welcoming washed over him. He heard a small cry from inside the room. Anna had Remka's Light and it had her.

Higley had heard Anna's cry and knocked on the door. "Are you alright?" he asked, opening the door.

Anna had her back to the door, so no one could see her face. "Yes," she said. "I'm fine. I was just reading a very touching note from my aunt. It choked me up. May I have a minute more?"

"Of course," Higley said, closing the door.

"It's been quite a day for her," the bank manager said.

"Yes, it has," Higley agreed. "I think that it would be best if she went back to the hotel and rested. She has a lot of decisions to make over the next few days."

The door opened and a transformed Anna walked out.

"Are you alright?" Higley asked.

"Yes," Anna said. "I just wish I'd known my aunt. She must have been quite some lady."

"It was my father who dealt directly with her but from what I remember I believe she was indeed quite a lady," Higley said. "Might I ask what was in the box? You don't have to answer. I'm just being nosey." He smiled at Anna.

Anna smiled back and took a small, carved, wooden box out of the handbag Helen had bought for her. The carving was rich and detailed. Rollie knew that it was very old and likely from the Black Forest region of Germany. She opened it and pulled out small, silver pendent. It was a pentagram, not the amulet Anya had described.

"Well, that's odd," Higley said. "Just a small pendent. Doesn't appear to be valuable."

"It had value to Aunt Anya," Anna said. "She wanted me to have it. She had it stored so it wouldn't become lost. Her letter explains it."

"Well, the box is an antique, so it has some value," the bank manager said. "But, I think that the real prize is the letter. A link between you and your ancestress."

"Yes," Anna said. "If there is nothing else, I'd like to go back to the hotel. I'm a bit tired."

"Of course, my dear," Higley said. "Helen has some things she needs to take care of but I'm sure Rollie will be able to stay with you."

"Yes, that's fine," she said.

Rollie helped her pick up all of the documents pertaining to her money and put them in her bag. She replaced the carved box and thanked both Higley and the bank manager. She gave Helen a hug, then turned to Rollie.

"May we go now?" she asked.

Rollie opened the door and stood aside to let her out. They were shortly in the car and Rollie started to drive to the hotel.

"Why didn't you tell me?" she asked.

"Tell you what?" he asked. "That you were rich? Helen told you that yesterday."

"Don't play games with me," Anna said. "I know who you are. You're a wizard, or a sorcerer or something. I knew when I touched that thing."

"What thing?" he asked.

"The thing my aunt left for me," she said.

Rollie turned off the main street into a residential neighborhood. He found a place to park and stopped the car.

"Let's start from the beginning," he said. "Tell me what was really in the box."

"It had two things," Anna said. "The pendent I showed to Mr. Higley and another item. It was a copper piece with a blue stone in the middle. I've never seen anything like it. I picked it up and something happened."

"Tell me," Rollie said.

"I felt a kind of shock, like finding a friend you haven't see for a long time," she said. "Then, I saw a glitter begin to grow inside the stone. I almost dropped it but I couldn't. I suddenly seemed to see everything clearly for the first time in my life. It was like I could see the thing within the thing. I know that doesn't make sense, but I can't describe it. When I stepped out into the office and I looked at you, I saw you for what you really are. You have a power, or something you call on to help you help people in trouble."

Rollie was startled. Remka's Light was more powerful than he'd guessed. The power of untold generations of Wielders must be locked inside for her to be able to see not only that he was gifted, but also how he used those gifts.

"Wow," Rollie said. "That's some kind of amulet. I knew it was powerful, but it and you surprise me." He paused to let Anna realize that she'd been correct. "I guess it's time to come clean with you," he said.

"So start with who you really are," she said.

"My name really is Rolland Jones," he said. "I work with a group dedicated to the Powers of the Light and who try to keep Wielders, Guardians and their focuses from falling into the hands of the Dark Ones. Wielders, like you, are those who have the ability to use a focus to perform acts, manipulate things. Guardians are those who are not able to directly use a focus but are charged with keeping them safe and seeing that they are passed on to a Wielder. We call ourselves the Butler Knights. One of our leaders is a seer and she received a Sending that a Guardian was in danger. It turned out to be your great, great aunt Anya."

"You mean she's still alive?" Anna asked.

"Yes, she is," Rollie said. "And, she's waiting for you to come to her so you can help her find her way home." He told Anna an abbreviated version of Anya's rescue and how he and Miguel had been sent to protect Anna.

Anna was silent for several moments. "Good grief!" she said. "This sounds completely insane. How do I know this isn't some weird scam to get your hands on my money?" she asked.

"The amulet knows," he said. "What's it telling you?"

She put her hand over her heart and closed her eyes. "You're a good person," she said. "But, I feel that there's something you need me to do. What is it?"

"My partner, Miguel, is the man found in your apartment," Rollie said. "You know how you've been worried about him. That's your power. You're a healer. And now with Remka's Light, you have the means to help him. Will you?"

Anna thought for another minute and then nodded her head. "I don't know what I can do, but let's go to him," she said.

Rollie drove to the hospital, but didn't immediately get out of the car. "They won't let us enter his room without approval from the police detective," he said. "I have a way to keep people from noticing me. It's a spell. I know it works for me but I don't think you could perform the incantation. You don't have any training and also, it's tied to my ring and not your amulet"

"You mean that the amulet might not let me cast your spell?" she asked. She suddenly laughed. "Listen to us. Talking about casting spells like trading recipes. I should be terrified thinking that I've gone crazy, but you know what? I think I'm finally getting a glimpse of who I'm supposed to be."

"I know," Rollie said. "I went through the same thing no so long ago. Takes some getting used to." He thought a moment. "Here's an idea. If I cast the spell while holding your hand, it might envelope both of us."

"We can try," she said, holding out her hand for him to clasp.

"Lean in close," he said.

Rollie took a deep breath and looked into his ring and letting power flow into it. He took her right hand in his left then held his right hand over both their heads and began to chant. As he finished, the green from his ring washed over both of them. Anna sat back and put her hand over the amulet. It felt warm, as if it had powered up. She looked over at Rollie. "I don't think it worked," she said. I can still see you."

"That's normal," he said. "It really only works on people who don't work with the Power. But, people can still hear us and feel us if we touch them. Also, remember that we're not really invisible. It's just that people won't notice us, especially if we aren't moving. So, when in doubt, freeze."

Anna nodded and got out of the car. Moving carefully, they made their way to the reception desk. Rollie guessed that they would have moved Miguel to the hospital proper by this time. He needed to find out where and that meant checking the computer. He had Anna stand next to the wall while he waited for his chance to look into the computer files. He only hoped that he could find what he needed quickly.

His chance came when the volunteer manning the reception desk left to go help a discharged patient with their bags. Rollie moved quickly to scan the computer screen. It was a complex system, but he took a chance and had it perform a search using Miguel's name. A second screen pulled up showing Miguel's room number and a warning that no visitors were permitted. Rollie noted the room number and closed the screen just before the volunteer returned. He retrieved Anna and they headed for the elevator bank.

There was still a police officer outside of Miguel's room. They'd need a distraction, but what? Anna pointed at a cart holding empty meal trays and dishes. Rollie grabbed the cart and tipped it over. It made a satisfying crash that brought all kinds of people running, including the officer.

Rollie and Anna entered the room. Miguel was laying on the bed looking much as Rollie had seen him in the emergency room.

"Miguel?" Rollie asked, again. "Can you hear me? I have Anna with me. She has Remka's Light and wants to try to heal you. Try to help her. By the Rod, harm to none."

Anna stood next to the bed and looked down at him, a frown of concern drew her eyebrows together, but her voice was very soft when she spoke. "Hello Miguel," she said. "I'm Anna and I want to help you but I'm not sure what I'm supposed to do."

Remembering Anya's story of how Remka cured the village children Rollie instructed her to duplicate what Remka had done. "Place your left hand over his forehead and hold the amulet in your right hand, then let the Power flow."

Anna looked nervous, but did as Rollie suggested. Nothing happened for several moments, then a blue, glittering light began to shin deep in the middle of the stone. Just like Anya had said, it ran up Anna's arm, across her breast and down the other arm to flow into Miguel's head.

The flow seemed to continue for a long time. Rollie began to worry about how long Anna could sustain the flow of power. She'd never done it before. She might do too much and burn out. He was about to interrupt her when the light faded. Anna staggered back from the bed and would have fallen if Rollie hadn't caught her.

"Hello, Anna," Miguel said, opening his eyes. "I'm Miguel. Thank you for healing me."

Rollie grinned and hugged Anna who was crying in relief.

"I take it that I'm in a hospital," Miguel said.

"Yeah," Rollie said. "And, you're under arrest for burglary and vandalism. There's a police officer guarding your room."

"Okay," Miguel said. "And how did I get here?"

"You were found unconscious in Anna's apartment. You were badly beaten. Do you remember who did it?

"All I remember is seeing a dark shadow enter Anna's building after she'd left to catch the bus. I guess I should have followed Anna but I decided to find out what the shadow was up to. I remember feeling heaviness like with the fog on the dock. I couldn't move. Someone or something tackled me and then nothing."

"Look at your ring," Rollie said.

"It's dead," Miguel exclaimed. "How?"

"That's for the Ladies to determine, but I'm guessing it's something the Baron cooked up," Rollie said.

"Then we've got to get Anna away from here," Miguel said. He tried to sit up, but fell back into the bed. "Maybe in a few minutes," he said.

"Can you come up with a feasible story for the cops as to why you were in Anna's apartment?" Rollie asked.

Miguel grinned and nodded.

"Okay, then I'll get Anna out of the area," Rollie said.

"Wait a minute," Anna said. "Don't I get to have a say in what I do? I mean, if I just up and disappear, Mr. Higley is going to have every law enforcement organization in the country looking for Rollie and me. And, you'll never get out of jail."

"She's right," Miguel said. "We need to create a false trail, something like she's decided to take a long vacation and wants you to go along for protection. It's not really that far from the truth."

"Sounds like a plan," Rollie said. "If you agree, that is." He nodded at Anna.

"Yes, but I need to have a long overdue discussion with my parents first," she said. There was a new gleam in her eyes that made Rollie feel that her parents were in for a rude awakening.

"You better be going," Miguel said. "I'm guessing that these sensors will show that I'm awake and someone will be coming to check on me."

"Take care, brother," Rollie said.

"You, too," Miguel said. "Now get going."

Rollie heard footsteps approaching the door and flattened against the wall. Anna followed his lead so that both were unnoticeable when a nurse opened the door, followed by the police officer. They exited the room and hurried down the hall. Again, they had to be careful to not bump into anyone, so it took some time to reach the car. Rollie reversed the spell and drove away.

"I hope Miguel will be alright," Anna said. "I mean with the police holding him."

"You don't need to worry on that account," Rollie said. "He's been doing this type of thing for some time. He'll get away with no one the wiser. Right now, we need to come up with an explanation that will satisfy Mr. Higley."

"Why not use the idea Miguel suggested?" Anna asked. "I've decided to take a vacation so that I can think things over and want you to go along for protection. Of course, that might make him think you were a fortune hunter."

Rollie didn't understand at first then he did and blushed. "I hope you don't think any such thing," he said.

Anna laughed at his discomfiture. "I think that if you were, Remka's Light would zap you."

"You're probably right," he said.

Chapter Seventeen: Fleeing to Milan

Rollie took Anna back to the hotel so she could rest. Between the shock of finding that she was rich and acquiring the amulet, then drain of using power for the first time, she was exhausted. While she slept, Rollie began to make plans for them to leave the city. Anna was correct when she said that they just couldn't vanish, much as Rollie wanted to do just that. No, they'd have to make their departure public, at lease on the surface.

Anna slept through to the next morning and was very hungry. "I feel like I could eat the entire breakfast menu," she said.

"I know," Rollie said. "That's a side effect of using the Power. Many focuses retain the power of their prior Wielders for the current ones to draw on, but power also comes from within you. It's draining, especially when you aren't used to doing it. I don't know how the Ladies manage to do all the arcane things they do without burning out or eating the ship's galley bare. But, they were born to it and trained early. Must make a difference."

When they had finished eating, Anna picked up her handbag and headed for the door.

"Where do you want to go today?" Rollie asked.

"First, I want to go to my workplace," Anna said, somewhat grimly. "I have a few things to say to Mr. Pace in addition to I quit."

Butler Knights weren't supposed to get pleasure out of conflicts, but Rollie had to admit that he wanted to hear what Anna said to the jerk and it was everything he'd hoped. Anna told Pace that he was a bully and he didn't deserve to have employees of the caliber that she and Irene were. There was no excuse for his treatment and he was just afraid others would see him for the loser he was. She grabbed a small figurine from the desk she'd worked at, tucked it into her bag and walked out the door, back straight and head held high. Rollie wanted to cheer.

"That went well," he said when they got in the car. "Where to next?"

"My parents' house," she said. "I'm going to let them know that I'm not the stupid girl they've always led me to believe I was. I have my own life and the means to live it and I'm going to."

Rollie nodded but hoped she wouldn't burn her bridges like he'd done with his parents. He didn't know what to say or if he should say anything. It was her life, as she'd noted. He sighed and asked for the address.

The interview with her parents was every bit as bad as the one with his had been. There was shouting and name-calling and Anna left the house in tears with her father following.

"Go ahead," her father shouted. "Go off with your gigolo boyfriend and see what happens. But, don't come whining to us when he leaves you broke and someplace you can't get away from."

"Let's go," Anna said to Rollie. He held open the door, keeping an eye on George in case he decided to get physical. A curtain hanging in an upstairs window moved and Rollie saw a dark form. A Dark Hunter was in the house. Every hair on his head stood on end. They needed to get out of there fast.

Rollie sped away from the house and headed back to the city, but not directly to the hotel in case they were being followed. Anna had been softly crying and not paying attention to where they were going. When she finally looked up, she seemed confused. "Where are we?" she asked.

"I need to be sure we aren't being followed," Rollie said. "There was a Dark Hunter in the house. We need to get away from here and right now!"

What's a Dark Hunter?" Anna asked.

Rollie had been debating about telling her, but decided she needed to know. "Dark Hunters are creatures of the Dark Powers and are at the command of their emissaries. They create chaos and are often deadly carrying out the orders of the servants of Darkness."

"Are my parents in danger, my mother?" Anna asked, concern reflected on her face.

"Not now," Rollie said. "They're after you, not your parents. There appears to only have been the one. Its presence in the house was most likely the reason for your father's anger. They have that kind of influence over the non-gifted."

"No," Anna said. "He's been like that for as long as I can remember. Always angry, always, I don't know, condescending and hateful. I've never understood how my mother has stayed with him."

"Maybe you'll be able to help them when you come fully into your power and are trained to use it," Rollie said. "The Ladies will be able to help you with that."

"Do you really think so?" she asked, a pleading look in her eyes.

"It wouldn't surprise me," Rollie said. He'd been wondering how long her father had been under the Dark Hunter's influence because he had no doubt that was the case. They must have been waiting for the day when the amulet would reappear and like Miguel had said, they were stationed near anyone with the family name. He almost shuddered to think how much danger Anna had been in growing up. It also may account for how meek she'd been until she took possession of the amulet. Had there been more than the one Dark Hunter, he doubted they'd have made it out of the house. "The sooner you get trained, the better for all concerned. We need to make our getaway. Is there anything you need from your apartment?"

"Well, clothes for one thing," she said. "But, I don't know what to take. Where are we going?"

"Milan," Rollie said.

"Italy?" Anna squeaked. "I don't have anything to wear in Europe and I don't even have a passport."

"You can buy clothes anywhere," Rollie said. "I suggest that you meet with, no call Mr. Higley and tell him about your desire for a long vacation. Maybe you could tell him how your stressful meeting with your parents was and that you want to let things cool down. Ask if he could recommend someone to close up your apartment as you are leaving right away. As for a passport, I'll show you how to enchant a small notebook to become one. It's one of the few spells I can do without really thinking. I have no doubt that Miguel has already escaped and that the police will have contacted Mr. Higley. Your safety will be his paramount concern. I can tell him that I'll travel with you as your bodyguard. But, under no circumstances tell him we are going to Milan. Anna nodded but looked doubtful.

They arrived at the hotel and found Helen waiting. "Where have you been?" she asked. "The police called Mr. Higley and said that the man from your apartment had escaped custody. We were very concerned when we couldn't reach you by phone."

"I asked Rollie to drive me to my parent's house," Anna said. "I needed to tell them about my inheritance and what it means for me. My father wasn't pleased, to say the least. He wanted me to turn everything over to him so he could take care of me, as I wasn't capable of doing so myself. Needless to say, the discussion went downhill fast."

"I'm so sorry," Helen said. "It's a big adjustment. Likely things will calm down after he's had time to think."

"I hope so, but I'm not going to put up with him harassing me," Anna said. "You and Rollie both asked me what I'd like to do now that I have funds and I've been thinking about it. I'd like to take a long vacation and experience some different cultures. Do you think Mr. Higley might be able to help me make arrangements?"

"I'm sure he could," Helen said, "but are you saying that you want to go soon? "I'm not sure it's wise to leave just now."

"Well, I'll discuss it with Mr. Higley," Anna said. Then, as if it was a startling idea, she looked at Rollie. "Perhaps, Mr. Jones could accompany me for protection. Would you be able to do that?"

"Well, I don't know," Rollie said. "I'd need to check it out with the office. There are some pending cases. Let's check with Mr. Higley and see what he says."

Helen nodded her approval of Rollie's statement and phoned Mr. Higley. He wanted to talk with Anna in person and asked her to come to the office. Twenty minutes later, the four of them were sitting in his office.

"Anna, my dear, I appreciate your desire to want to do something new and exciting, but I must recommend that you take some time to really think about how your circumstances have changed and not go off half cocked. Take things slowly so you know that what you do is good for you."

"I appreciate your advice and I know it's sound," Anna said, "but after this morning's fight with my father, I know that I need to get away and find some perspective. Also, Helen said that the man from my apartment had escaped. I don't want to be imprisoned for my own safety any more than I want having my father take over my life again."

Mr. Higley looked at Anna for several moments. He must have seen her resolution, for he nodded his head.

"You've got a good head on your shoulders, Anna," he said. "I don't think you'll be foolish and maybe getting away will be best. But, I don't think it's a good idea for you to be wandering around by yourself in strange countries. So, my condition for helping you to get ready is that Mr. Jones accompanies you. If not him, then Mr. Lennox, when he returns."

"That sounds just fine," Anna said. "How soon can arrangements be made?"

It was nerve wracking to wait for Higley to make reservations for them. He was methodical whereas Rollie wanted to grab Anna's hand and dash to the airport. Instead, they had to wait until the next day. The Dark Hunters were closing in. He could feel it. The only good thing was that Miguel was around. He'd met with Rollie in their hotel room while Anna and Helen were asleep. Rollie filled him in on the plan to get Anna out of town. Miguel would do what he could to help, but he was still weak.

"Maybe we should call the Ladies," Rollie said. "At least we can let them know we have Anna."

"I'll give them a call," Miguel said. "You'd better get back to Anna. If you even think there could be a Dark Hunter nearby, grab her and run. Never mind trying to keep cover. Just be ready to defend Anna."

Rollie nodded and went back to the suite. Anna was sitting on the sofa waiting for him.

"Are we going to be killed?" she asked.

Rollie wanted to tell her that everything would be fine, but he couldn't. "The situation is very dangerous," he said. "The moment you took possession of Remka's Light, the Dark forces became aware of you. They will be coming after you with every resource they have."

Anna looked completely terrified and Rollie wanted to say something to comfort her but she must learn the truth of her situation.

"Can't the amulet protect us, me?" She asked.

"If you were trained in its use I don't think any Dark Power could stand against you. But now, you are basically a lure and our best chance is flight and not fight. I don't know if it will be possible, but we'll just have to try."

Anna didn't say anything but pulled the amulet out and stared into the blue stone for several moments. Her eyes widened and she looked up at Rollie.

"Rollie," she said. "The amulet has gone bitter cold. I think we need to leave right now."

Rollie too had felt an unease growing. Something evil was closing in on them. "Get dressed," he said then whirled to face the door. Miguel slipped in.

"You sensed them," Miguel said.

"Yeah," Rollie said. "As soon as Anna is dressed, we'll get out of here."

Anna came back in and picked up her purse. "What about Helen?" she asked.

"We'll call Higley when we're someplace safe," Rollie said. "But we can't wait to make explanations now. Let's get going."

They left the suite and took the elevator down to the parking garage and got into the car. Rollie drove to the airport but instead of going to the car rental agency, he chose one of the garages attached to the terminal. He hoped that being indoors with lots of bright lights would help to keep any Dark Hunters from directly attacking them. However, he wasn't able to find a space near an entry into the terminal. They'd need to walk the entire length of the garage.

When he opened the car door, Rollie immediately sensed that something was wrong. In spite of being at a very busy airport, there were no people around. The roar of the jets was muted and the air felt heavy.

"Okay," he said to Anna. "They're here."

Anna looked at him, fear in her eyes. She could sense them, too. "What do we do?" she asked.

"Start walking," Miguel said. "Keep your eyes open and if I say to run, run."

Anna nodded and looked around before beginning to walk toward the doors into the terminal. They'd gone about halfway before six Dark Hunters appeared in front of them. Like black mists in shadows, the

Dark Hunters surrounded Rollie and Anna, cutting them off from Miguel. A growling chant began that was painful to hear.

Rollie held his ring over Anna's head and tried to perform a spell of protection but he felt the power in his ring begin to fade. Without thinking, he reached out to take Anna's hand and felt the power from Remka's Light swirling around her. He grabbed it as he would a lifeline and fed the power through his ring. As he'd heard Umar at the dock in New York, he voiced the command, "Angamiza!" Green fire flared and the Dark Hunters were hurled away clearing a path.

"Come on," he gasped, hauling Miguel to his feet. "Run and don't stop for anything."

It took only seconds to finish crossing the garage but it seemed much longer. They were breathless when they entered the terminal.

"We're safe," Anna said.

"Don't count on anything, yet," Rollie said. "Keep your eyes open and tell me if you sense anything."

Anna nodded and took hold of Rollie's hand again. They headed to the airline-ticketing desk and proceeded to make the ticket purchases needed to get them to Milan. It took time, but eventually they were able to work things out.

The flights were uneventful for which Rollie was thankful. Anna had never flown before and was anxious about the trip as well as about being stalked by the Dark Hunters. Rollie discovered that being both the extractor and protector meant he needed to be hyper-vigilant. He hoped that they could rest on the flights but he found that he couldn't. He kept looking at the other passengers as they passed by and wondered if any were in league with the Dark forces. He was relieved when they finally arrived in Rome.

"So, what's next?" Anna asked after they left the airport. Dark circles showed beneath her eyes and there was a droop to her shoulders that told of her exhaustion. Had he known it, Rollie was in a similar condition.

"I called the ship and spoke with Mr. Pierce," Miguel said. "We're to take the train to Milan. The Ladies will send a car to meet us and take us to a safe house where we're to meet up with them and your aunt. Then, we'll see what they have planned."

It took a little over two hours to reach Milan on the high-speed train system. Anna was almost too tired to be interested what she saw as they sped through the country. Rollie hadn't been in Italy before, so Miguel described the sights.

"Oh, I hope I get to come back and really see Rome," Anna said. "When I'm not so tired."

"I'm sure you will," Miguel said, "and the rest of the country, too. There's much beauty and history to explore."

Rollie knew that Miguel would keep watch, so he felt that he could close his eyes for a few minutes. He was surprised when Miguel nudged him awake just before they arrived in Milan.

As arranged, they were met by a car and taken to a large house near the center of the city. A set of marble steps led up to an impressive door that was opened by a butler as they reached the top step.

"Welcome, Sigorina Steadman, gentlemen," he said in a light Italian accent. "The family and Signora Steadman are waiting for you in the salon. If you will please follow me."

He led them down a shot hallway to a set of dark wooden doors and knocked then opened the door.

Chapter Eighteen: The Gathering of the Forces

"Are you sure about this, Agnes?" Sofie asked as the three sisters and Anya stood in front of the elegant house situated on a quiet Milan street. They were plainly exhausted. They had used the time under the Power travel spell to make their plan to defeat the Baron. They also had taken care of Nolan when he dropped the spell. The number of increments he'd spent as the locus of the Power travel spell was greater than they'd attempted before. He'd finally collapsed the last time the spell dropped and the Ladies felt it was their responsibility to help revive him. Dr. Quan had taken over his care while Gordon Pierce took the Happenstance into the port of Genoa.

"Okay, Ladies," Pierce had said. "We're docked. The captain should be up and around soon, so I'll be ready to go whenever you say."

"I thought we'd told you that you were going to sit this one out," Agnes said.

"That was for Miguel and Rollie's assignment," he said. "This is different. You'll need protection."

"Protection?" Sofie exclaimed. "What are you talking about?"

"This Baron character you told us about," Pierce said. "You said that he was the most powerful Dark sorcerer you'd ever heard of. That he'd murdered your grandparents and almost killed you mother and father and they had the help of the Rod of Compassion. You don't want to encounter him without backup I think that with myself and three or four of the others, we should be well covered, especially if Umar, Miguel and Rollie show up."

"Gordon," Caroline said. "We appreciate your concern, but,"

"But nothing, Miss Caroline," Pierce interrupted. "Until the captain returns to duty, I'm in charge of the ship and crew. I won't stand by and let you put yourselves in such danger without aide."

"Yes, your duty is currently to the ship," Sofie said. "But that stops once we leave the ship."

"Our protection is in speed and stealth, not letting the world know where we are by forming a parade of people," Agnes said, her face red with emotion.

"Yes, but," Pierce started.

Agnes finally lost her temper sent a shower of sparks across the lounge, melting a glass decanter. "You were saying, Mr. Pierce?" she asked through gritted teeth.

"Agnes!" Caroline exclaimed. "Stop! Gordon is only showing he cares. He's not demeaning our powers. He'd never do that." She turned to face Pierce, a pleading look in her eyes.

Pierce shook his head, obviously not happy, but realizing he couldn't win. "All right, Miss Agnes," he said. "But you must promise me that if you don't get the help you expect from your parents that you'll send for a team. Promise on the Rod."

Agnes' face was still stormy, but Sofie and Caroline both nodded. "All right, Gordon," Caroline said. "You have our promise."

"By the Rod?" Pierce asked.

"By the Rod," Sofie said. "Right, Agnes?"

"I'd forgotten how much steel you have in your spine, Mr. Pierce," Agnes said. "Very well, you have my promise. If we don't get our parents' help," Agnes said.

The end result was that the women arrived in Milan agitated and very short on sleep.

"Dad was pretty insistent that they'd retired the last time we spoke," Caroline said.

"I know, but they can't leave us standing out on the curb with a guest in the middle of the night now can they?" Agnes said. "It would be rude. Besides, I'm much too tired to take no for an answer." Agnes climbed the steps and rang the doorbell. Shortly, a middle-aged man dressed as a butler opened the door. His eyes widened in surprise but he swiftly admitted them.

"Signorina Agnes, Signorina Sofie, Signorina Caroline, Madam," he said, bowing slightly to each.

"Good to see you, Antonio. Please let them know we're here and are waiting in the drawing room," Agnes said. "Also, we'll need some food, tea and plenty of coffee."

"Si, Signorina," Antonio said, again bowing the ladies into the large, tastefully decorated room and closing the door behind him.

"Whatever it is, the answer is no," a man's voice said from the opposite side of the room. He stood up from the deep chair he'd been sitting in, finger holding his place in a book he'd obviously been reading. He was tall with silver hair and deep blue eyes that looked out from a creased, tanned face.

Agnes grimaced and opened her mouth but Sofie cut in.

"Hello, Dad," Sofie said. "Let me introduce Miss Anya Steadman. Anya, this is our father, Kenneth Butler."

"How do you do, Miss Steadman?" he said, stepping forward to shake her hand.

"Mr. Butler," Anya acknowledged his greeting. "I hope you will forgive this unexpected intrusion."

"We need help, Dad," Agnes finally said.

"We've had this discussion before. Your mother and I are retired and you girls are on your own. You've got your coven, your Knights or whatever you call them. You have all the help you need," he said.

"It's the Baron," Caroline said. "He's escaped."

A crash made everyone jump and turn to the door. A small woman with grey streaked red hair stood swaying amid broken china and splattered coffee. The tray she'd been bringing dangled from her fingers before dropping to the floor.

"Mother," Sofie cried, rushing to keep the woman from collapsing and helping her to a chair.

"Celeste," Kenneth said, coming to her side, "Take some deep breaths. Do you need a healer?"

"No, I'm fine," Celeste said. "It was just a shock."

"Yes," Kenneth said, glaring at the other women. "Caroline, how could you upset your mother like that? It wasn't funny."

"No, it wasn't," Caroline said, "and it wasn't a joke. The Baron has escaped from the Nothingness you sent him into. He's after Anya and her great grandniece, Anna, and one of the most powerful focuses we've ever heard of. He wants to gain access to Sanctuary."

"He couldn't," Kenneth said. "Sanctuary's protections are beyond even his abilities, great as they are."

"He could, if he gets his hands on the amulet, on Remka's Light," Agnes said.

"Remka," Celeste said, frowning in thought. "I've heard of a great mage called Remka, but she lived centuries ago."

"Yes and Anya was Guardian to her amulet and Anna is the current Wielder," Sofie said. "You must have felt something when Anna took up the focus. We certainly did thousands of miles away and if we did so must have the Baron. He will be after her with his Dark Hunters like bloodhounds on a scent."

"No," Kenneth said. "We can't help. We cast him into the Nothingness and sealed the portal to imprison him. It took everything we had even with the Rod of Compassion. The effort killed your grandparents and drained your mother until she almost died, too. We have nothing more to give. You can't ask us for more."

"We have no choice," Celeste said. "We are sealed to the Power of Light and even if it means our deaths, we must stop the Baron. He will destroy this world to get to Sanctuary and from there, how many other realms will he devour? We cannot hide from this."

Kenneth's shoulders slumped as he accepted his wife's words. "Do you have a plan?" he asked his daughters.

"Yes," Agnes said. "We open the portal into Nothingness, send the Baron so deeply into it and seal the portal so tightly that he'll never escape and we ask Remka and those dwelling in Sanctuary for help to do it."

"Help from Sanctuary? How?" Celeste asked.

"We use Remka's Light," Agnes said.

They sat late into the night discussing the plan that the Ladies and Anya had come up with. Having gone up against the Baron before, Kenneth and Celeste provided what guidance they could.

"An untrained Wielder, a few of your coven members, us and only a hope of help from those who've gone to Sanctuary against one of the most powerful Dark mages ever to live doesn't exactly inspire confidence in your plan," Kenneth said. "But, I can't think of any better ideas. When do you expect your Knights?"

"Tomorrow at the latest," Caroline said, eyes staring at the fist-sized globe she'd been holding. "We need to send cars to meet the train from Rome for Mr. Jones, Mr. Valdez and Miss Steadman and to the hospital to pick up Mr. Kambuto and his party."

Caroline pressed her lips together and looked at her parents. "I think we'd better explain about Mr. Kambuto," she said, "or more truthfully, about those he's bringing."

"Oh? And what is it about these guests that you've not mentioned?" Kenneth asked, looking hard at his daughters.

"He's bringing Herr Gustav Vogel and his personal assistant," Agnes said. "They're Nazis, or at least Herr Vogel is and he's been working with the Baron. They know about Remka's Light and what it's capable of. Herr Vogel has been under the Baron's influence and Mr. Kambuto has had to keep him incognito as a dementia patient for the past couple of days"

"I'm going to bed," Kenneth said, walking out the door.

"I think we all should get some sleep," Sofie said. "Tomorrow is going to be a busy day."

First to arrive was Umar, Karl and Gustav Vogel. Vogel was conscious and cursing both Umar and Karl as they carried him into the house. Sofie cast a sleeping spell over him and had the men carry him to one of the bedrooms.

"He'll sleep until we release him when we get to Freiheit Dorf," she said

"Freiheit Dorf is where Herr Vogel claims to have seen his miracle," Karl said. "According to the Swiss records, it was destroyed by a massive landslide."

"That's true, but we're not going to go looking for the village," she said. "We're going to find the portal to Sanctuary."

"But, that's exactly what Herr Vogel has wanted for most of his life and what he promised the Baron in return for help," Karl said. "You can't want them anywhere near that place."

"Oh, but we do," Sofie said. "We most certainly do."

Later in the afternoon, Rollie, Anna and Miguel arrived. They were shown into the salon where Anya waited.

"At last," Anya said, rising from the chair she'd been sitting in. She looked intently at Anna who was staring back at her.

"Anna," Rollie said, "this is your great, great aunt, Anya Steadman."

Anna stepped toward Anya who raised her arms and gathered the young woman to her. Rollie watched, smiling at the reunion then backed out the door when Miguel touched his shoulder indicating they should give the women some privacy.

"The others are in the drawing room," Antonio said, opening the door.

"Miguel, Rollie," Agnes said. "Well done."

"Miguel, are you alright?" Sofie asked. "Your ring is drained and you're injured. Do we need to send for Dr. Quan?"

"I'm fine," Miguel said, "but the Dark Ones have a way around our protections."

"They learned from my encounter with them on the dock," Umar said. "I used the ring's power in conjunction with an incantation of my own to stop them. I'm sorry that it left you open to them."

"No, it was a spell devised by the Baron," Agnes said. "Miguel's and Rollie's rings were impaired before you made your casting."

"Well, at least we know what they're capable of," Sofie said. "We can't count on using our standard protection spells."

"So, what do we do now?" Rollie asked.

"The Baron is much too powerful for just us, so we'll need help," Agnes said. "We need Remka and Anna will have to open the door to Sanctuary for us."

"But, Anna isn't trained to use the amulet," Rollie protested. "Her healing Miguel was instinct, not knowledge. She could be killed."

"What is it you need me to do, Miss Butler?" Anna asked as she and Anya walked into the drawing room.

"We need you to use Remka's Light to open the portal and call Remka to help us," Caroline said. "Anya saw what her mother did and will be able to coach you. The rest of us will combine our talents and provide a protective barrier against the Baron and his Dark Hunters. We'll ask Remka to help us send the Baron back into Nothingness and seal the door so that he will never again be free to roam this world."

"But, what if Remka refuses to come and help us?" Anya asked.

"Then, our world is lost," Celeste said.

"Miss Steadman," Kenneth said, "Do you truly understand what you're being asked? It will be your burden to use the amulet and it may well kill you. But, it isn't just risking your life. If we do not succeed, if you do not succeed, the Baron will gain control of Remka's Light and then he will become unstoppable, draining the life forces of every being on this world, then moving on to the next and the next and the next."

"Father!" Sofie said.

"No, she must understand so that she makes an informed decision," Celeste said.

Silence enveloped the room as each person thought of the fight to come. Anna took the amulet from around her neck and gazed into the depths of the glittering, blue stone.

"I think," Anna started, "I think this is why Remka left the Light here in this world. She knew that the people would need its protection. It chose me to wield it's power so whatever happens, I must see it through."

"Then, we'll get ready to leave for Switzerland," Kenneth said.

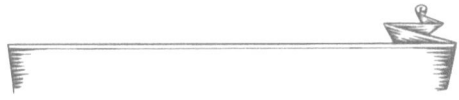

Chapter Nineteen: Portals of Light and Dark

Twenty-four hours saw the group ready to leave for Freiheit Dorf, rather for where it had been. Sofie and Celeste put Herr Vogel into a trance state where he could be handled by Karl and Umar. Once in Switzerland, they gave the impression of being on a tour and looking for their ancestors' old home. This brought considerable cooperation from locals, especially when Anya spoke with them of her girlhood memories.

"I never knew anything about you or my great grandfather coming from Switzerland," Anna said. "No one ever spoke about it."

"I'm not surprised," Anya said. "George always blamed me for losing our mother. Once I left his house, I realized how verbally abusive he had become. I'm sorry that this trait was passed down and you were subjected to it."

"It wasn't your fault, Aunt Anya," Anna said. "Rollie thought that my father was that way because of the influence of a Dark Hunter."

"No, he is because his father learned it from my brother," Anya said.

"Rollie also said that when I'm fully trained to use the amulet, I might be able to help him. I'd like to and my mom, too. Can you tell me anything about using the amulet?"

"You already know about how Remka used it to heal the village children," Anya said. "You used it yourself to heal Miguel."

"Yes," Anna said. "Rollie had me use the amulet like Remka did to heal Miguel. Although, I think that it used me more than I used it. But didn't your mother ever tell you stories about how she or her ancestors used it? Maybe how her mother trained her? Didn't she ever give you any beginner's exercises or have you read an instruction manual?"

Anya laughed at Anna's questions. "That's not how it works," she said. "Magical training isn't like going to a class. It's a one to one relationship between teacher and student for lack of a better description."

"Could you tell me whatever your mother told to you?" Anna asked, eagerness showing in her face.

Anya was silent for a long time then she spoke in a very soft voice. "I was only three or four when Mama began to teach me how to breathe," she said. "Learning to breathe is very important. Let me show you."

The two women spent as much time as possible talking. Anna began to see Anya as heroic and her heart filled with love and gratitude for all of the sacrifices Anya had made to keep her safe.

It became a grueling trek once they started into the deep Alps where only hiking trails existed, as they didn't dare use the roads too much. Herr Vogel's wheelchair was sturdy enough to be pushed and pulled by the men over the rocks, but Anya wasn't strong enough to climb. Rollie and Miguel devised a carry chair for her after Anna's offer to use the amulet to help was vetoed by the Ladies.

"We don't want to call the Baron before we're ready for him," Agnes said, "and using it would be like a beacon drawing him and his Dark Hunters."

So, the group made their way slowly, ever deeper into the mountains. They stayed in cabins and huts when possible, but camped out under the open sky when other shelter wasn't available. Finally, Anya looked up at the peaks and pointed at a gap opening between two of them.

"This I remember," she said. "This leads to the valley. My brother and I came this way after the village was destroyed. We should be there before noon."

"Good," Kenneth said. "It'll give us time to rest and get ready."

"How long do you think it'll take for the Baron to catch up with us?" Anna asked.

"That's going to depend on several factors," Celeste said. "We may have days or only hours. We'll just have to take it as it happens."

Anna sighed and started trudging behind her aunt's carry chair, wincing as a cold breeze flowed out of the gap they headed into. The amulet seemed to become heavier with each step. It was as if it recognized where they were going. It felt like it was pulling power from the very earth, growing until Anna wondered if it might drag her to the ground or explode. Perhaps all that power would destroy her, as well as the Baron. She tried to stifle a whimper but Rollie heard it and turned his head to look at her.

"I think what we're feeling is a test left by the spell that opened the portal," he said.

"A test? Anna asked. "What for?"

"To see if we have the will to continue and that our intentions are for good," he said.

He smiled and she could tell he was trying to give her some of his courage. A stubborn streak bloomed within her heart. If the others could walk blindly toward an unknown fate, so could she. She'd volunteered, after all. Or had Remka's Light volunteered her? That was something to think about.

The group continued to trudge for what seemed like hours. Anya wouldn't have made it if she'd been forced to walk.

"We're here," Agnes suddenly shouted from the head of the line. "Can you feel it? The entire valley is awash with Power."

Anna most certainly could, but unlike the burden she'd been feeling, this was a release, a support, and a welcome. The amulet was warm against her breast and she could sense that it was glowing, ready to... to what? Anna didn't know, only that she was the conduit and was ready for what was to come.

Anna turned and walked toward the blank face of one of the towering cliffs that overlooked the valley. She was drawn to it. She felt Anya's hand take hold of hers and glanced at the old face that was staring at the rock wall.

"Yes," Anya said. "It was here that we gathered. The families were standing together, touching each other for comfort but silent, waiting. The only sound was the breeze hissing as if flowed over the grass. Then the little clink as Mother touched the amulet to that flat stone and spun it like a coin. And it was there that the portal formed and we saw the land beyond." She pointed to the base of the cliff. "And it was through there that the people left and where Mother was pulled in. The last time I saw her. It's been a long, long time."

Anya swayed and Anna wrapped an arm around her shoulders. Rollie came up with the chair and placed it next to the flat stone. He handed Anna a package of food and a canteen of water. "Try to rest while we get set up," he said. Both women looked back and saw that the others were forming a large circle on the ground with small stones gathered from the avalanche debris field.

"These stones were bathed in power from opening the portal into Sanctuary," Celeste said, noting Anna's interest. "We'll form a pentagram using myself, Kenneth and the girls as the star points. Rollie, Miguel and Umar will stand outside of the pentagram to guard the circle."

"We'll combine our powers and form a shield while you use the amulet to open the portal," Caroline said. "Hopefully, Remka will answer your call and will grant us aid."

"What if I can't open the portal?" Anna asked. "I don't really know how to use the amulet. I might not be able to get it to work."

"You will, my dearest one," Anya said. "When the time comes, you'll know what to do. Just remember to breathe."

"But, what if Remka doesn't come?" Anna asked. "What if she won't help?"

"Anna," Caroline said. "You are the Wielder of Remka's Light. You cannot permit its power to be stolen by the Dark forces. You must either use it to cleanse the Dark or keep it from ever getting into their hands."

Anna understood what Caroline meant. Either the Baron was destroyed or the amulet was and herself with it. The momentary fear of that thought was suddenly replaced by the soothing warmth emanating from the amulet and with it, a calm sense of purpose. She nodded her head and sat down next to Anya to wait for what was to come.

The afternoon sun was beginning to drop behind the western mountains before their preparations were completed. Herr Vogel's wheelchair was pushed next to Anya's chair and Karl sat next to him on the ground. Sofie came up and stood in front of them.

"We'll need to release him now so that we may concentrate on our defenses. Can you handle him?" she asked Karl.

"Yes, but he'll rage at everyone," Karl said. "Will that distract you?"

"No, but you must keep him away from the circle and not let him interrupt whatever Anna does," she said. "As he's been under the Baron's influence, he'll be open to manipulation so be on guard. Sit on him, if you must."

Karl nodded and Sofie stood in front of Herr Vogel, chanting to remove the spell. Herr Vogel swayed and blinked as one coming out of a sleep.

"What.. what happened?" he asked. "Karl, what have you done?"

"I've tried to save you, mien Herr," Karl said.

"You fool!" Vogel exclaimed and tried to rise from his chair. Karl was kept busy trying to restrain him.

Sofie went back to the circle and took her place at one of the star points that formed the pentagram. Umar and Miguel were on either side of the circle, acting as side guards to prevent any Dark hunters from slipping by. Rollie stood next to Anya and Anna to guard them should it be needed.

As the sun dropped behind the mountains, the moon rose over the eastern peaks. A handful of stars began to shine in a sky deepening from bright blue to a clear, sharp midnight blue. The air was chill and clean with the fragrance of the meadows surrounding them. Breathing deeply, each felt the power of the valley fill them with strength.

As if one, each person's head turned to the gap in the southern wall of the valley. Shadows flowed out of the gap, man shaped but filled with a malignant force reflected in their yellow eyes. They spread out, forming a protective ring. Finally, like a dirty brown cloud, a mist appeared and became solid. The Baron stood and gazed at the defenders in front of him.

The Butlers had engaged their powers and the circle and pentagram glowed as if made from polished silver. They chanted their spell of protection and a column of bright, white light formed in the middle of the star. Without thinking, Rollie held out his hand as a fist, his ring pointed toward the Baron. He reached with his own gift to link with Umar and Miguel and them to each other forming a triangle of green light. Karl was still struggling to keep Gustav in his wheelchair. The old man fought with a strength Karl did not realize he possessed.

Anna stood with Anya and listened to the whispered words only she could hear. Soft and warm, she was told what she needed to do. She took the amulet off from the chain around her neck, breathed on it and held it up to capture the light of the moon and stars, then she stooped and spun the piece. Glittering motes of blue light began to gather and swirl into the blue stone at the center of the spinning amulet. More and more the power of the valley gathered until Anna and the entire valley was bathed in blue light. She opened her arms to gather the light and as her ancestor had done, she flung the power at the rock wall.

Slowly, a tunnel appeared in the wall and light grew on the other side. A green meadow appeared and with it, two women walked toward the portal. One was tall and blond with a strong, proud face and the other, petite and dark yet equally strong. The blond woman stopped but the dark woman continued through the portal until she stepped through. Remka once again walked in the world.

"You have called me," she said. "I have come. What is it you need of me?"

Anna felt as if she could no longer speak. Awe at the power of Remka made her feel as if she should fall to her knees yet the need of this world made her point at the Baron standing beyond the Butlers' barrier of light.

"So, Remka," the Baron said. "You've left Sanctuary and come to meet me."

"No, Baron," Remka said, "I was called to help those who have chosen the path of Light. Never will I serve the Dark or you."

"Is that so?" the Baron asked. "Then let us test which is mightiest." He reached out and gathered a handful of shadow that lengthened into a shining, black staff. He slammed the staff onto the ground and a shockwave of energy flung the Butlers off their star points like a wind scattering autumn leaves. The circle and pentagram dimmed and the Baron strode across where the barrier had been, stopping only when he reached the green light stretched between Umar, Miguel and Rollie.

Remka had come forward and placed her hand on Rollie's shoulder. He felt her power flow into him, strengthening the force built between him, Umar and Miguel.

"You cannot pass, Baron," Remka said. "You are barred from Sanctuary as you knew you would be when you pledged fealty to the Dark. No matter what happens to us, here, you will never get what you really want. You threw it away."

"You are wrong, woman," the Baron said. "Once I have your amulet I will have all the power I need to access Sanctuary and the worlds beyond. You cannot stop me."

"Very well," Remka said. "Try to traverse the portal. None here will stop you."

Remka removed her hand from Rollie's shoulder and the green light faded. Rollie, Umar and Miguel stood as if frozen in place. The Baron, wary of a trap, made a gesture to test his path to the portal. Nothing happened. Stepping forward, he waved a hand at Karl and sent him flying away from Vogel.

"Up, old man," the Baron said and gestured Vogel to stand and walk in front of him. When they got to the portal opening, the Baron shoved Vogel into the tunnel. There was a blinding, blue flash and Vogel disappeared, only a trace of dirty, grey mist was left to dissipate in the air.

Meanwhile, Remka had again placed her hand on Rollie's shoulder and the green triangle of light reformed. Rollie could move again. Almost as if he pulled the knowledge of what to do out of thin air, Rollie made a similar gesture as Anna had done to open her portal and threw the triangle against the cliff wall next to where they stood. An opening formed. Blackness such as no human had ever seen formed the core of this portal. Bitter cold flowed out, touching each living creature within the valley walls, seeking, drawing those of the Dark back into the void.

The Baron, seeing his Dark Hunters disappear approached the Sanctuary portal, his staff held in front of him. As with Vogel, there was a blinding flash when the staff touched the opening. The staff dissolved and the Baron was flung back landing next to Anna.

"You are answered, Baron," Remka said. "You are barred for all time. Go into the void of Nothingness as is your fate."

"No, Remka," the Baron snarled, foam gathering at the corners of his mouth. "If I am barred, so will you be."

The Baron turned and made a grab for the amulet, still spinning in a core of blue light.

"No!" Anna cried. "It's not yours and you can't have it."

Rollie suddenly reached out and grabbed at the blue light, flinging it at the Baron. As the light touched him, the Baron screamed and was lifted from his feet. The bitter cold from the void wrapped around him and pulled him inside. Rollie made another gesture and the green triangle shrank, closing the portal then his hands closed together and the glittering from Remka's Light sealed the entrance leaving only silence. It was a silence so intense that it seemed time had stopped.

"Awaken, all of you who are sealed to the Light," Remka said, her voice ringing like a crystal bell, breaking the oppressive quiet. The Butlers stood up and rushed to hug each other while Umar, Miguel and Karl all stepped forward, smiling at one another.

"The Dark has been defeated, thanks to all of your efforts," Remka said. "As long as there are those who will risk all for the sake of right, the Light will always prevail. Now, decisions must be made and partings endured. What say you, my children?"

Anya looked at the woman who had remained in the realm of Sanctuary. "Mama," she said. "I should have gone with her, but if I had, this night would not have happened and the Baron would have remained in this world. I have long felt guilty that my act to save a doll made George stay, but perhaps, it's what needed to happen."

"Indeed," Remka said. "And you have the wisdom to realize this. Your mother has waited for you and you are free to join her and your friends." Remka motioned for Anya to go through the portal.

"Aunt Anya," Anna said, choking with emotion. "I'll miss you."

"Oh, my dear," Anya said, hugging the young woman, "go and live your life. Pass on what you learn and keep to the path of the Light. Know that you are much loved and always will be." She reached up and wiped a tear from Anna's cheek then turned and walked toward the Portal. "You take care of our girl, Rollie," she said, looking back over her shoulder. Rollie could only nod his head.

An old woman stepped into the tunnel, but a young girl appeared on the other side and ran to her mother's waiting arms. They waved farewell to those looking at them, then walked across the green meadow and out of sight.

"And now, another choice needs to be made," Remka said, turning to face Rollie. "Even though you are not fully come into it, you have the power of a mage within you. You have the right to be called a brother and will be welcome to enter Sanctuary. But, my time here is coming to an end and we must be swift. What is your choice, to come or to stay?"

"My place is here, in this world," he said after only a moment's hesitation. "I'm pledged to the Light, with 'Compassion for All and Harm to None'."

"Then I will say that you have made the right decision," Remka said, smiling, "I foresee much adventure in your life ahead. Go in peace, my children."

"Lady Remka," Anna said. "What of your amulet?"

"It is yours now," Remka said. "Use it well." She turned and walked through the portal. As she stepped back into the meadow, the portal dimmed and closed.

As happened before, the blue light from the amulet grew until it was blinding, then shrank back into the stone. This time, only a single gong rang out over the valley, then there was just the sound of the breeze swishing over the grass.

Chapter Twenty: A New Knight and A New Mage

"Well, it's time we left," Celeste said. "Let's get gathered up. I don't really want to spend another day here."

Everyone looked up and realized that the sky was growing light. It didn't seem possible that so many hours had passed. They gathered up what they'd brought with them and went back through the gap. It felt as if they were stepping out of a world that no longer existed. The trails didn't seem so difficult to traverse as they had coming in. The group unexpectedly came upon a road they hadn't seen before and where they were able to flag down an intercity bus. It didn't seem to take long to reach a town with rail service and they bought tickets to Bern, then on to Milan. Once they were back in the townhouse, they all collapsed and slept.

The next evening found them all seated at the large dining table. They had a celebratory feast but were still wound up from the battle and the part each had played. Only Kenneth and Celeste had been through something so intense and knew it was necessary for the others to talk about it. Finally, they calmed down and became quiet.

"So, what's next?" Sofie asked.

"We need to get back to the ship," Agnes said. "I called Captain Nolan earlier. He's back to himself. He and Mr. Pierce have secured a cargo. Since we're all okay, he wants to get underway. We were so far ahead of schedule other ships are getting backed up waiting to dock."

"What are your plans, Karl?" Kenneth asked. "Now that Herr Vogel is no more."

"I've been on the phone to the Vogel corporate office letting them know that Herr Vogel has died," Karl said. "Per his instructions, he was cremated and his ashes will be scattered at the park named for him in Munich. I will bring the urn and as his only heir, scatter his ashes myself. No one will ever know what really happened. Not that anyone would believe it if I told."

"What of yourself?" Celeste asked.

"I will continue to run Vogel Enterprises, but with differences," he said. "There is much need in this world and much which can be done with our resources to help. I hope that if there is ever anything that I can provide to further your organization's goals, you'll let me know."

"Thank you, Karl," Caroline said. "Thank you."

"What about you, Anna?" Celeste asked. "Will you go back to the States and your family?"

"I don't think so," Anna said. "I thought I had better call Mr. Higley. He was pretty livid. I could hear it in his voice. He was about to contact Interpol and report me missing and accuse Rollie of being a kidnapper. I told him that I decided to take a cruise on a tramp freighter for an extended period of time. You see, I have this gift and I need to learn how to deal with it. I was basically letting it use me back at the valley and from what Aunt Anya said I don't think that's the way it's supposed to work. I need to find a teacher. Do you happen to know of one, or three?"

Agnes, Sofie and Caroline all smiled at her.

"We'd be happy to welcome you as a Knight in training," Agnes said. "Especially as it appears that we'll also be training a new mage, won't we, Rollie?"

Rollie looked startled, then confused. "But, I'm a Knight, not a mage," he protested. "I don't have a focus, just my ring for protection. It was Remka's doing back in the valley."

"You're wrong, Rollie," Miguel said. "Think about what you did when we were looking for the P.I. back in Denver. That spell of compulsion came from within you. And look how you grabbed power from Remka's Light to fight the Dark Hunters in the parking garage. You even used a word of command from Umar's culture. You shouldn't have been able to do any such thing with just a protective ring."

"It was you who linked us to form the triangle of protection in the valley and it was you who opened the portal into the void," Umar said. "It was also you who used our combined power to send the Baron into it and then you used Remka's Light to seal the door. You have the Power, believe it."

"It's true, Rollie," Caroline said. "A mage's power comes from within them. They don't need a focus. But, that doesn't mean that one might not come to you so be aware."

"All right, then," Sofie said. "Let's plan to get back to Genoa tomorrow and find our next project."

"We already have one," Caroline said. "I received another Sending. There's a young boy who may have come under a severe curse," Caroline said.

"Where?" Agnes asked.

"Florida," Caroline said.

"Isn't that where Jay asked about going a few months ago?" Sofie asked. "Something about a jade figurine recovered from a shipwreck?"

"Yes, and I don't think it's a coincidence," Caroline said.

"Huh," Sofie said. "Looks like we have our sailing orders. We best get ready to go. Does anyone need anything? We won't have much time before we'll have to catch the train tomorrow."

The next morning, everyone said goodbye with many hugs and promises to keep in touch.

"And please, please remember," Kenneth said, "Your mother and I are retired."

"But Dad, it's such a waste," Agnes started to say, then saw everyone else was grinning. "Well, we'll see."

The End

About the Author

While born in Utah, Belenda L. Tonge has spent the majority of her life in Colorado. Earning a Bachelor's degree in accounting from Metropolitan State University of Denver, she became a technical auditor and retired as an operational supervisor in the energy industry.

Belenda loves to bake, enjoys a variety of music, likes to watch old black and white mystery movies from the 1930's and 1940's and avidly reads science fiction/fantasy, adventures, mysteries and historical fiction.

"Remka's Light" is her first novel and the first book in a planned series, 'The Butler Knights'. She still resides in Denver, Colorado under the benign dictatorship of her four-footed housemates.

About the Publisher

Belenda Tonge is the publisher of the Butler Knights Quest series of books.

.

.

www.ingramcontent.com/pod-product-compliance
Lightning Source LLC
Chambersburg PA
CBHW021104130626
46554CB00002B/521